Love, Peace, Joy and... Harmony

AIRADAS SIVAD

DEDICATION

I dedicate this writing to God. Thank you! Thank you for the gift. Thank you to all the great people I've met along my journey. Aunt Lilly, you are my Angel. Our conversations are priceless. Mary Monroe, one of the BEST authors ever. You're right, "God Don't Like Ugly." Thank you for encouraging me to write. To my "verbal first drafts" (everyone I vented too), I apologize. To D.J. A.K.A. "King of the Keys" and the only person I've ever met that lived "that" traumatic event. I shared my experience at eight, but I didn't share about the second time it happened at 21. Yes, I lived it TWICE. Almost identical situations (you're lucky you got away; I was not as fortunate). Your strength gave me the courage to keep going. Though we met in passing, the music will live on.

Lastly, to anyone I ever hurt, forgive me. Writing freed me to forgive anyone I ever felt hurt or betrayed me. Life is to short not to forgive. I'm learning how to love, live, and laugh.

Contents

ACKNOWLEDGEMENTS

To God be the GLORY HONOR and PRAISE!!

PREFACE

Thank you for your support. Now go read about: Love, Peace, Joy and... Harmony.

INTRODUCTION

$\mathcal{T}$hank you for calling. How may we pray with you today?" the representative said.

"Um…hi, well…I'm calling to pray for my family," the voice stuttered, shaky. The representative could almost taste how unsure the person behind the phone was.

"Yes, how can we pray?" the representative inquired.

"Yes, my family is…well, different." A pause. "They desperately need prayer."

"And exactly who needs prayer?" the representative asked.

"Well, there's Joy," the person started. "She's the eldest. She's a church fanatic. She frequently gives unwanted advice, which she rarely takes herself. See, Joy is overweight; she focuses on others to avoid facing her issues. Joy is desperate to get married. She often meets losers who abuse her." The caller waited to get some sort of response from the representative, but when she got nothing, she continued.

"And… well, there's Peace. Peace is the youngest sister; she's friendly, outgoing, and peaceful. Men love her because she's needy and beautiful. She enjoys playing dumb. However, she excels academically."

"She's finally ready to complete grad school. See, Peace avoids drama at all costs unless…her family needs her."

"Quite a family you got there, ma'am," the representative interrupted the caller, amusement playing in her voice.

"Now, don't let me start on Love," she continued. "We call him L; L is the youngest. L and Peace are almost a decade younger than their siblings. L is very social, and girls love his charming demeanor—L is naïve. He believes everyone is his friend; he can be irresponsible and relies on his sisters to get him out of trouble. He ignores their advice if it does not align with his beliefs."

"Oh, I see. Are there any other siblings?" the representative asked curiously.

"Well, ahh…yes. There's Harmony. Harmony is a diva! She believes all should kiss the ground she walks on, and doors should swing open at her mighty presence. If it's not about Harmony, it's irrelevant! She's a passionate intellectual." The caller beamed.

"However, she refuses to commit to anything. Her goal is to be rich! Sadly, by seeking rich men, she's made bad decisions in relationships. But… she is optimistic that she will meet her other half…one day. We…I mean they, just need prayer," the caller finished, catching short breaths after her long epistle.

"Let's pray. Father God, we pray for divine instruction for this family," the representative started.

"Lord, may they find comfort in their time of need; let them be lights to your kingdom. God, we ask you to bless them abundantly. And—" The quick 'click' sound of a call coming to an end filled the caller's ears.

"Hello? Hello? Aargh, this phone," the caller hissed.

Chapter 1: All Eyes on Me

$\mathcal{P}$eace, where's your sister?" Joy lifted her head from her chocolate caramel cake and fussed. They had been waiting for their sister for an hour; had eaten, and were on dessert.

"Now, Joy, you know she couldn't be Harmony if she didn't walk in at least forty-five minutes late." Peace threw her head back, bubbling with laughter. It was her idea to have them meet in that particular restaurant, as it was Harmony's favorite.

Joy vented, taking a bite of her cake; her thick arms flapping with every swing. "She always must be fashionably late; I just don't understand." She nodded at the waiter, requesting if the bill should be served.

"You know your sister; it is what it is." She shrugged and continued typing away on her phone.

"I just—" Joy began, but was interrupted by the sound they knew too well.

"The Queen has arrived—you may refrain from applauding, please." She beamed, a wide smile playing on her freshly glossed lips as she checked her finely manicured nails.

"Lord, Harmony, not today," Joy said flatly, rolling her eyes.

"Joy, are you going through the change? I mean, really, you should smile more. With all that frowning, you'll need Botox by spring." Harmony chuckled, taking a seat.

"With all the work you've had, I know who NOT to go to," Joy snapped, a bored, expressionless look on her chubby face.

"And what's that supposed to mean?" Harmony opened her mirror to her face, touching it slightly.

"Now, you two, please." Peace sighed.

"Is it my fault I'm envied by many?" Harmony shrugged. "Just once, I'd like to walk in a room and not have everyone stare. Aaah, to be me…well, it could be worse. I could be over 200 pounds and lonely. Joy, what's it like? You know, sleeping in an empty bed and not being able to tie your own shoes?" Harmony's chestnut eyes narrowed, a small smile on her lips.

"That does it! Let me tell you something," Joy bellowed.

"Joy, ignore her, you know she's off!" Peace shot a deadly glance at Harmony.

"Harmony, stop! That's not why we're here. Joy has something she wanted to ask you. Go ahead, Joy and Harmony." She gave her a quick warning glare. "Be nice."

"Hmph, what do you need now?" Harmony asked, feeling self-important.

"Need?" Joy let out a dry laugh. "I've never asked you for anything. Let's remember you slept on my couch and filed chapter seven, or did you forget?" Joy paused, lifting her head up.

"You know I'm better than that. Lord, forgive me. I will not let this child take me there." Joy took a deep breath and continued, "Well, the reason we're here is to talk about a domestic violence event. The sponsors wanted you to speak about Cousin Giovanni." Joy paused. Silence filled the room; the awkwardness could slice flesh open.

"Sorry, Joy." Harmony's voice came out small and soft. "You *know* I don't like to talk about that. Besides, it's too soon," she said quickly, looking away.

"Harm, it's been almost ten years. Her story might deter others from being in the same mess," Peace persuaded, squeezing Harmony's hand softly.

"Ten years...hmm, it still feels like yesterday; still can't believe it. Honestly, I just started living my life. So, I really don't want to go backward," she said plainly, not looking at either of them.

"You, you, you; it's always about you. Just once, can you do something for someone else?" Joy paused to catch her breath. "Please, we really need you to speak at the church."

Harmony rolled her eyes. "Now, you know I don't do church."

"You know… you need to get over stuff and learn to forgive," Joy said.

"Exactly! I couldn't agree more …. So, I'm taking your advice and getting over things. Have fun at your event," Harmony said plainly and walked out.

"Harmony, wait," Peace called out, her eyes heavy with concern for her sisters. "Joy, really, you know how she is." Peace reached out for Joy, but she looked away.

"Well, I'm sick of walking around on eggshells to please her," she complained.

"She needs to grow up and get a life!" Joy took another bite of her third dessert, causing Peace to sigh mentally.

"She won't even speak about her own family to help people out, because of what happened with her and a crazy Pastor. Just because SHE trusted a pimp in a suit, now we all gotta suffer? Pathetic," she sassed.

Peace's face fell. She understood both of her sisters, but she knew that Harmony could put forth effort and Joy could have more compassion.

"Let's give her some time; she'll come around. I gotta head back to class," she said, gathering her black backpack and rainbow-colored notebook. "I'll call you later. Love ya." She grabbed her phone and eased herself out of the table.

"Love you, too," Joy replied with a cross face, causing Peace to smile warmly at her. "Stay clear of those men!" she called out, raising her hand helplessly.

∞ ∞ ∞

"I make one mistake, and everybody keeps bringing it up," Harmony muttered under her breath, throwing herself into the car. They can sleep around with everything moving, have twenty baby daddies, but if they're in a pew, they're fine? Damn right, I'll never step foot back in a den of hypocrites."

Harmony's tears busted forth like angry water from a dam. She looked towards the window, desperate for somebody to lend her a helping hand, to save her. She clasped her hand on her face as she drowned in her own tears, raw from the inside.

"God, I know you're in control, and I forgave everyone, but it still hurts. I keep feeling like it should have been me. I mean, everyone loved her. God, she had no enemies," she cried out. "I was the one people hated to see coming. I was so hateful! I blame myself… I should have done more."

Her eyes enlarged with tears, as she felt her walls crumbling. "I just can't talk to a church full of people. God, every time I walk into a building with a pulpit, I think about being locked in that room. Not knowing if he was going to kill me or if anyone would hear me scream."

"Who does he think he is to just treat women like that?" she choked out, slamming her balled fists into the steering wheel.

"He was supposed to be a man of God. For him to say I would be cursed if I didn't sleep with him," she paused to wipe her nose. "God, I know this is just a test." Harmony stole a quick glance at the mirror.

"Harmony get a hold of yourself. You're a diva and divas don't cry. Everything is ok. You're perfect! Whew… God, I'm not trying to go there. You brought me out, and I know you're in control, so I know it will all work out. God, continue to order my steps. Lord let no anger rise in me. In Jesus' name, I ask and pray. Amen." She wiped the remaining tears, and strapped her seatbelt on.

"Perfect timing, looks like Joy's calling for round two." A small, almost evil smile played on her lips as she brought the phone to her face to answer Joy's call.

"What, Joy?" she spat.

"So, you just gon leave?" Harmony could taste her signature eye roll through the phone. "You need to grow up!" she said, trying not to upset Harmony.

"You're calling my phone to argue with me?" She sighed as she saw a girl pushing a guy towards the restaurant. That, and Joy's accusing tone, angered Harmony further. "Apologizing is what you should be doing."

"Fine, you want an apology? I'm sorry. I'm sorry you're such a selfish, bougie, broke, wannabe diva that can't get off her high-horse to help no-body!" Joy yelled into the phone.

Harmony's eyes narrowed; Joy was hitting a nerve. "Apology accepted. Now, go eat a Twinkie, big girl!" Harmony said, then put an end to the call, letting out a dry laugh. She was proud of herself.

Voice message from Joy' the phone displayed. She checked her voicemail. *You ungrateful thing. I know you didn't just hang up on me. Big Girl? No, you didn't, after all the lypo you had. If I weren't saved, I'd be at cho' front door when you got home. Don't nobody hang up on Joy. You know what, you gon need me again and when you do…DON'T ASK ME FOR NOTHING!*

"Guess I'll power my phone off to avoid any more psychos calling," she muttered. Harmony chuckled, as she switched her device off. She shoved the phone into her bag and geared the car into motion.

∞ ∞ ∞

"Finally," Harmony murmured under her breath, as she dropped her bag on the console table. In a swift move, she eased out of her heels and plumped herself on the luxurious finely imported Eichholtz Cesare Sofa.

Harmony loved her posh home. The sophisticated furniture, high ceilings, and sparkling chandeliers made her feel aristocratic.

She proceeded to check her mail, and then moved to her answering machine.

Mmh…Hello, Harmony. It's your cousin, Alexandria. I knew you probably were out, but since I don't have your cell anymore. I thought I'd try this number. Well, my business partner needed XL's number. He has a big show, and he wanted to book him. Call me back!

"Hmm…I bet. I wish this sociopath would get the hint."

Hello, this message is for Har-mon-y Wentworth. Yes, Ms. Wentworth, this is Ms. Anderson from JNC Bank. I still need to speak to you about your account. It's urgent! Call me today at 212-555-3432. Thank you.

"Hmm, urgent my... wait on it."

Hello, Stranger. The voice came out sexy and deep. *This is Kwame. Haven't heard from you in a while; Call me. The number's still the same.* The beep erupted from the machine again.

"Did everyone wake up with me on their mind?" she muttered, picking up the phone.

"Hello, Alexandria," she said with a straight face.

"Hey, Cuz! How have you been?" Alexandria beamed

"First, we are *not* cousins," Harmony said flatly.

"Even though we're not," Alexandria paused, "I still consider you family. How have you been?"

"Busy." Her face was as straight as her reply.

"I bet. So, how's the family?" Alexandria asked coolly.

"Fine." She rolled her eyes. That call was the last thing Harmony wanted to be doing.

"You still work downtown? I know you make a killing now." Alexandria was trying to keep the call as lively and familiar as possible, but Harmony was having none of it.

Harmony took a deep breath before saying, "Alexandria, what did you call for? I'm extremely busy."

"Hold on, y'all *betta* sit *cho'*... I know you didn't. Y'all STOP MAKING ALL THAT NOISE! Wait till I get off this phone." Harmony couldn't fight a small smile from forming on her lips; she knew Alexandria was at it with her kids again.

"Harmony," she returned to the call, "be glad *cho' ain't* got kids. Girl, you know I *love* my kids, but they be trying me. I can't wait to take a break from them. Anyways, my business partner wants to do a show with XL, and I was wondering if you could give me the number to his manager, so we could book a show?"

"Alexandria, I'm not going to call his manager. He doesn't have time to play games," Harmony said, a bit crossed.

"Nah, Harmony, this is serious. We *bout* to be paid! We got plans," Alexandria beamed, in the happiest, most enthusiastic tone she could muster.

"Well, put your business partner on the line." Harmony knew Alexandria would have continued till she obliged.

Harmony walked impatiently to the kitchen, as she waited for Alexandria to respond.

"Oh, Okay. I'll conference him in." Harmony sighed, taking a sip of her apple juice, as she got comfortable on her Italian sofa.

"Hello? You there, Harmony?" Alexandria called out. If she knew something about Harmony, it's that she could have dropped the call.

"Yes, I'm here," she replied, sounding bored and uninterested. Annoyed that Alexandria was taking too long, she pulled her dark chocolate flowing hair into a messy bun.

"Harmony, this my business partner, Tore." Alexandria beamed.

"Hello, Harmony. I've heard so much about you."

"Uh-huh." She finished the bun and returned to the call. "Hi, explain the event?" She went straight to the point. It was in no way a meet and greet.

"Yo," Tore's raspy voice filled Harmony's ear.

"I would like to book Summer Jam with XL. Yo, Mac, Don-Da, Queen Lyrica, and Freddy Fire confirmed. XL would close the show. Lexi said you had his contact info, so I'm callin."

"Lexi?" Harmony shot a brow up. "Who's Lexi?" she questioned. She found Tore's upbeat voice a bit annoying.

"Harmony… that's me, silly." Alexandria let out a stiff, uncomfortable laugh.

"Oh, okay. Well, Tore, this is their livelihood. They do not take kindly to games."

"Yo, Miss, I am not playing games. This is my business. I do this on a regular. It's also my livelihood."

"Well, Tore, give me your number. I will tell them to call you."

"Thank you," he said happily. "It's 212-555-2422."

"Ok, I'll let them know. Goodbye," Harmony said flatly, removing the phone from her ear.

"Thank you again.," Tore chirped.

"Bye, Cuz."

"Why am I getting involved in this drama?" Harmony fumed, as she ended the call without responding to Alexandria.

"Alexandria is the biggest liar in town. Wish she would stop telling people she knows me." She sighed in mock helplessness, as she downed the remnant of her apple juice and started channel surfing.

"Lexi." She let out a burst of dry laughter. "She done went from Alexandria to Alex to Lexi. Now that's when you know you're trifling. Continually making new aliases." She laughed again, as she settled on CBN, plopping both of her feet on the couch. She picked her phone up, and pushed some buttons.

"Talk to me.," the deep voice erupted from the end of the phone.

"Hey, Platinum."

"Harmony? Is this you?"

"You know it is. The one and only." She laughed, raising her hand up. "How you doing?"

"Good, you know, XL was just talking about you."

"Oh, he was?" Her throaty laugh filled Platinum's ears. "He must have known I was calling; that man has radar."

"You know he does when it comes to you."

"N-E-ways. How's your family?"

"Oh, they good."

"Awesome. Well, the reason I'm calling is, Alexandria's business partner wants to do a show with XL," Harmony said, her voice a bit shaky.

"Hell No! Your lying cousin is full of it. All she does is lie and hoe. You know she slept with my guy's entire bachelor party, and she did it for free!"

"That girl is not my cousin." Harmony laughed. "I know she's scandalous. Dude might be legit, though."

"Well, call him back and get the info for us. Tell him to email the contract to me."

"What, now I'm your assistant?"

"Hey, when it comes to crazy...yes."

"Well, you need to put me on the payroll then." She threw her head back and laughed.

"Marry XL, and you will be."

"N-E-Ways. I'll have him email the info to you, nice talking to you again."

"You too," Platinum replied. "Don't be a stranger."

"I won't," she said, then ended the call.

"How did I get back mixed up with this girl?" Harmony mentally face-palmed herself as she considered what to do next.

"Dang, I'll just get the dude to email the contract, and that will be it," she concluded, as she dialed Tore's number.

"Hello, may I speak to Tore?" she said plainly, suppressing an eye roll.

"Speaking. Who is this?" he replied.

"Hi, this is Harmony; we spoke earlier." Harmony was seconds away from ending the call. Here she was, doing him a favor, but he was asking who it was.

"Yeah, Lexi's cousin!" He beamed.

"Aghh."

"Why you say it like that?" Tore's voice dropped; he didn't want to upset Harmony.

"She is not my cousin," Harmony spat out with an eye roll.

"Look, if you're on the *same-ish* she on and fronting, then let me know. Platinum is a professional. The last thing he needs is someone playing."

"I promise, I'm not playing."

"Well, if you are with Alexandria, you must be on something." Harmony couldn't hide it anymore, anybody that associated themselves with Alexandria, definitely had an agenda.

"Who is Alexandria?" he asked.

"You know, your business partner. Alexandria, Alex, and now she's calling herself Lexi." Harmony tried to suppress a burst of laughter.

"Business partner? Yo, you buggin. We are not business partners; I wish she would stop telling people that. I haven't talked to her in three years. I know shysty, but I remember her telling me that she had a "cousin" that knew XL. That's the only reason I called her. She played me and made me lose half a mil," Tore said bitterly.

"Well, I'm letting you know, I'm nothing like her, and I don't like liars."

"Me either."

"Glad we have an understanding," Harmony said, without any form of enthusiasm.

"In any event, XL's management wants you to email the contract. If they like it, they'll be in touch," she added quickly, not wanting the conversation to progress.

"Great! I've been trying to get this done *all* day."

"Here's the email; xlmgt@platinumrecords.com. Glad I could help. Goodnight."

"Do you always do that?"

"Do what?" Harmony asked, slightly pissed off.

"You know… rush off the phone."

"Goodnight sir," she said sharply, and powered the phone off.

∞ ∞ ∞

Joy walked into her house, a straight look on her face. What transpired between her and Harmony left her in the mood for no smiles or hugs.

The door swung open, revealing Misa and Miles; the children of a relative she agreed to raise. Misa was plopped on one of Joy's black sofas, while Miles sat on a beanbag, in front of the Smart TV. They arose to greet Joy.

"Hey y'all, did y'all eat yet?" Joy asked, not returning their hugs, as she removed both of her gray loafers, and eased into the couch, sighing.

"Yeah, we ate," Misa replied, running her hands through her freshly styled hair.

"Did you do your homework?" she said, taking a sip from the glass of water Misa placed on the table for her.

"Yeah," Miles replied energetically.

"Can we go over to Mrs. Rupert's house?" Misa whined, taking Joy's loafers from the floor. It always bothered her how her foster mother had huge feet. Mrs. Rupert said we could come over when you got home, if you said ok," she added.

"Did y'all clean up?"

"Yes. We did everything. Can we go?" Misa asked anxiously, twirling the hem of her purple t-shirt in between her index finger and thumb.

"Yes. Tell Mrs. Rupert I'll be over to visit in a bit," Joy said, with a small smile.

"Ahh, you're coming over? Why? We right across the street," Misa said anxiously.

"Yes, I'm coming over. What, y'all hiding something?" she shot a brow up.

"N-no, w-we're j-just ask-asking," Miles stuttered, stealing a glance at Misa.

"You know what? Let me call Mrs. Rupert," Joy fussed, and picked her phone up.

"No!" Misa yelled, shooting her hands up. "You don't have to call her," Joy fussed again, and then dialed the phone.

Love, Peace, Joy and... Harmony

"Hi, Mrs. Rupert, it's Joy. Fine and you? Good. Did you tell Misa and Miles they could come over today when I got home? Oh… I see… you haven't talked to them today. Not a problem. Mrs. Rupert, I have some business to tend to I'll talk to you soon. Thank you. Bye." Joy ended the call with a smirk and faced the children. They looked at each other desperately, like one was trying to urge the other to speak.

"So," she started. She shot a warning look at Misa, when she tried to take steps back. "You *gon'* sit there and lie to my face? After EVERYTHING I DO FOR YOU! What were you trying to do?" she asked furiously, her eyes widening.

"Nnn-nnn-nothing," Miles answered.

"Nothing," Misa said, without flinching.

"Y'all a nothing lie. Somebody better start talking, *now!* I'm not playing." She pointed a finger at them.

"Ok, we just w-wanted to h-hang out with our friends. Cause-Cause we didn't w-want to go to Youth Night. We're s-sorry." Miles clasped his hands together. He shoved Misa without Joy noticing. He knew she wasn't budging.

"So y'all lie to my face? You no-good heathens need-to-be-in church! Just for that, both y'all grounded. Don't ask me for *nothing!* Go to your room and get ready for church."

"But-but-but, I told the truth. Why am I g-getting grounded?"

"Boy, if you don't get out of my face. Lord, keep me," she yelled, making them scurry upstairs. Joy sighed, raising her hands helplessly. The kids took a toll on her.

"What you got to eat?" Ronnie walked into the living room, throwing Joy's car keys on the table.

He took a seat opposite her and stretched his legs on the coffee table.

Ronnie was the guy Joy settled for, after countless years of heartbreak. His overly tall figure, broad chest, plus his ugly goatee, wasn't exactly to Joy's specification, but she felt she had no choice. In her mind, marriage and a man was certainly overdue.

"I just got here. Did you forget something today?"

"No," he replied bluntly. Ronnie was a conman who only wanted Joy's money.

"You know, I had to walk home today."

"So, you needed the workout." He chuckled, pointing at her flabby arms.

"I'm *gon'* pretend you just didn't say that."

"Good, I'll say it again. So, you-needed-the-workout!" He chuckled again, this time, pointing at her legs.

"Why you got to be so hateful?" Her small eyes narrowed as she undid her necklace.

"Don't start that sensitive bull, I ain't in the mood. What you cooking? And don't say chicken." He clenched his jaw.

"Well, I got to go to the store. Hard to do, with no car and no money." She pointed at her keys on the table.

"What's that supposed to mean?" He straightened his posture, rubbing his goatee.

"Exactly what I said."

"Keep talking crazy," he said, as he returned to his formerly slouched position. "I wouldn't have this problem with Shellie," he mumbled under his breath.

"What!" Joy's eyebrow shot up. "Well, you go get with Shellie. She can have your out-of-work ass," she spat, pointing a finger at him.

"Who you talking to?" He sat up again. "Don't you ever disrespect me. Your fat ass outta be glad I'm here," he yelled, his eyes turning bloodshot.

"That's it." Joy swiped her keys from the table. "Get out!"

"I ain't going no damn where!" he yelled back, slouching back into position and plopping his feet on the table.

"Is ev-ev-everything ok?" Miles stuttered, peeking around the corner, shielding the living room from the stairs.

"We're fine," Joy replied without taking her eyes off Ronnie. "Get back upstairs, now!"

"You spend so much time focused on them badass kids." Ronnie chuckled, rubbing his goatee.

"Don't you talk about my kids," she spat, pointing an accusing finger at him.

"Your kids?" He burst into a dry laugh. "Your fat ass can't even have kids." He laughed again.

"I'm not *gon'* tell you again to get out of my house!"

"You make me leave. We both know as soon as I leave, you gon be calling me begging me to come back. Bet your church folks don't know I'm here. How bout I go tell them Miss Holier Than Thou is laying up with me and every other man she meets online?" He laughed again, throwing his head back.

Joy paused, the tears streaming out of her eyes. She struggled to wipe them off; Ronnie didn't deserve to see her crying.

"You a devil from hell!" She began to pray. "Lord, bind anything that's not like you from my home and cast it into the abyss. In Jesus' name, I ask and pray. Amen! Ronnie, you either can leave through the front door or through the morgue, but you're getting out of here!"

"You are threatening me?" He laughed.

"No, I'm promising you!"

"Forget you! You ain't even worth it! Don't be calling me back later, beggin," he said, walking towards the front door.

A loud knock on the door kept Joy from replying to Ronnie's narcissistic statements. Ronnie stood and strolled casually to the door, with a smug smirk playing on his plump lips. The door swung open revealing Peace.

"WHAT!" Ronnie scowled as Peace attempted to enter.

"What nothing, where's my sister?" She pointed her finger and walked past Ronnie. Ronnie and his faded brown shirt, plus his worn-out cowboy boots, didn't exactly please Peace.

"Peace, I'm in here," Joy said in a small voice, as she took her seat.

"You okay?" Peace asked, her voice laced with concern.

"Yes, everything's fine." She tried to form a smile, which faltered immediately.

"What you finna do?" Ronnie chuckled, as he ran his large hand over his goatee.

"Boy, you don't want none!" Peace removed her hand from caressing Joy's wrinkled forehead and edged up in Ronnie's face. Joy shot up immediately, restraining Peace.

"What you finna do? Bodyslam yo lil-"

"Bring it! You-sorry-mother... You better kill me! Put cho' hands on me!" Peace yelled, slapping Ronnie's chest.

The door swung open, revealing Harmony with a silver blade in hand. Miles pushed Misa to call both Harmony and Peace when the ruckus started. They knew, too well, how fights could get ugly in their home.

"I dare you. Do something! I'll cut cho' balls off! F-wit-me!" Harmony ran to the scene, blade in hand, with sweat dripping from her face. At the sight of the blade, Ronnie took a few giant steps back with his hands in the air.

"Y'all crazy!"

Joy grabbed the blade from Harmony, her sight squared on Ronnie. It was enough; he had made their sister suffer too much.

Harmony ran past Joy, tackled Ronnie and started beating him in the face.

"Harmony, no!" Joy yelled, as she tried to pull Harmony off of him, but Harmony persisted.

Peace took the vase from the coffee table, and in one move, clocked Ronnie in the head with it, causing the vase to shatter. Harmony cut loose, grabbed the lamp, and used the base to hit Ronnie in the groin.

"Peace, please, y'all *gon'* kill him!" Joy grabbed Peace, pushing her to one side.

"NOBODY'S GONNA HURT MY FAMILY AGAIN!" Harmony yelled, as she swung the lamp like Mark Maguire and knocked Ronnie out.

"Get back upstairs, *now!*" Joy yelled at Misa and Miles, as the sound of police sirens filled the house.

"Oh, no!" Harmony's eyes widened in horror. "I got a plan. We'll tell them he's an intruder. Peace, use a towel from the kitchen to grab a knife," she quickly added, realizing that there was no time for panic.

Harmony took her blade from Joy and hid it in the plant behind the door. Peace gave her the knife, and Harmony placed the knife in Ronnie's hand. She then messed up her hair and ruffled her clothes.

"Both of you, follow my lead. I'll do the talking." She motioned to Peace and Joy as she walked to the door casually. "Vincent Police Department." The bald man in a police uniform displayed his badge. Immediately the door swung open, revealing the three sisters: Harmony at the front, Joy and Peace behind her.

"Help us please! Thank God you're here." Harmony clasped her mouth with her hands. "This man tried to rob us." Tears fell from her eyes. "He, he has a knife. He rushed in and said he wanted money. Please, help us!" she added, the tears falling at a faster rate.

"Ma'am, it's ok, we're here now," the officer assured, with a small smile. "Is there anyone else in the house?" he added.

"Yes, my niece and nephew," she said in between sobs, as she struggled to wipe her pretend tears.

"We're going to ask all of you to go stand outside." The officer gestured for the door, as Miles and Misa walked into the room.

Harmony, Joy, Peace, Miles, and Misa walked out, giving the officer room to enter the house.

"He said he wasn't afraid of the police when I threatened to call. He said he'd killed cops before." Harmony turned around, pointing at Ronnie.

"Oh, he did?" The officer shot a brow up. "Ma'am, we have everything under control now; go outside."

Harmony nodded and walked out to meet the children and her sisters. She opened the car and motioned for them to get inside.

"What will my neighbors think?" Joy started crying, rubbing her eyes furiously.

"Joy, it's ok." Peace hugged Joy. After about five minutes of bawling her eyes out, Peace let go of Joy and closed the car door.

"Peace, we have to stick together on this one," Harmony whispered.

"Sis, I got you," Peace said, with a small smile.

"Go to Joy's car, and make sure he did not leave anything that can prove he knows her." Harmony knew her sisters well, and with that, she was sure she had to take control of the situation.

"Okay," Peace said calmly, as Harmony opened the door.

"Does he have anything in your house that can prove he knows you?" Harmony asked, facing Joy.

"Um… I don't think so," Joy said, in between sniffles.

"Stop crying," Harmony yelled. "I need you to think," she added, with an eye roll.

"No, he moved his stuff out two nights ago. He came back last night." She scratched her head slightly, as if the action helped her think. "Kids cover your ears," she yelled over her shoulder.

Miles and Misa quickly placed their hands on their ears; they knew better than to anger Joy at that moment.

"I called him last night; he took the car this morning."

"Did you give him anything that's yours?"

"He has my keys. No...wait, I got them back. No, I can't think of anything." She shrugged.

"Wait...no...my credit card!" Her head shot up, eyes wide in horror. "Sh--" Harmony paused. She was careful about what she said in front of the kids.

"Where is it?" she asked, as Peace opened the door and took a seat.

"Got everything," she waved the evidence in their face, "no traces," she said, feeling proud of herself.

"I don't know, probably his wallet," she answered Harmony's question.

"Broke mother...don't need a wallet. Are you sure he has it?"

"Has what?" Peace queried.

"Her credit card."

"I found it; it was above the visor; got the receipt in the cup holder too." Peace burst into a hearty laugh.

"Here they come; let me talk," Harmony said. She opened the door and stepped out. Harmony watched Ronnie stumble out with the police as she closed the car door.

"Would you like to press charges?" the officer asked notebook and pen in hand.

"Yes," she replied quickly, stealing a glance at Ronnie.

"Man, I didn't do nothing!" Ronnie yelled, as he tried to cut loose from the two policemen holding him. "This my girl house; they attacked me," he said, struggling in between the men. "Officer, thank God you got him; I fear for my life! He needs to be off the streets." She clutched her chest, throwing a wicked smile at Ronnie when the officer bent to take notes.

"Man, she's lying. *Crazy B*! I'm *gon'* kill you when I get out." He managed to release one of his hands, which he used to point at Harmony.

"Congratulations." The officer smirked. "You just earned yourself another charge."

"What? Man," Ronnie whined.

"If I were you, I'd keep quiet," the officer advised, with a chuckle.

"Damn!" Ronnie yelled, as the officers shoved him into the police car.

The officer gave Harmony the information on the court date, consoled her one more time, then walked to his car. Harmony said a quick thank you and waited for him to zoom off, before walking back to her family.

"Y'all good?" Harmony chirped, happy about how she took charge of the situation.

"Yeah, we're fine."

"Peace, take Joy and the kids to your house tonight. I'll clean up and bring their clothes over."

"Okay, Harm," Peace said, then opened the door to let the kids out.

"Nonsense." Joy raised her hands in protest. "I'm staying home. I have church tonight. Bishop got a program for the youth, I gotta be there." Her mouth parted into a small smile, to show gratitude. "Fine, have it your way." Harmony rolled her eyes at Joy, who in turn, shot her a warning glare. "I know you bet not bail his ass out," she muttered under her breath.

"What?"

Love, Peace, Joy and... Harmony

"You heard me, forget about him. He's not worth your time." Harmony embraced her sister, as she struggled to keep a tear from falling.

"I love you. No matter what we go through, you deserve the best." She tightened the hug. "And I'm not just saying that because you're my sister," she added and laughed.

"See," Joy laughed along, "she's back to herself. Love you, too." She pulled Harmony into a final hug.

"Me too, I love y'all," Peace said, a wide smile on her lips.

"Goodnight, y'all." Joy waved as she climbed out of the car.

"Night, sis."

"Night." Harmony waved, a contented smile on her face.

Chapter 2: This Too Shall Pass

The sound of Harmony's ringtone—something like a mixture of pop and techno—filled the air.

"Hello?" Harmony said, taking a sip of water—putting the phone on speaker.

"Are you supposed to be somewhere right now?" The voice came out irate and a bit familiar.

"Huh?" Harmony checked the clock and mentally slapped herself. "Agh, Juanita! I'm on my way," she said quickly, grabbing her purse, hitting the remote start on the leased Range Rover.

"Look, I like you," Juanita started, "but you can't keep coming in when you feel like it. Other people are going to think it's okay."

"I understand. I'm on my way," Harmony said sharply and quickly turned the phone off to get ready properly.

She grabbed the coffee off the table, turned the TV off, and closed the custom blinds.

Harmony caught a glimpse of herself in the mirror. She stared at herself for a while, touching her face at every angle. She always liked what she saw.

∞ ∞ ∞

The elevator doors opened, revealing an overly crowded office space.

At the side, stood a grand mahogany desk in a state of organized chaos. Two women stood in front of it, chatting.

"Oh, you're here? We didn't know where you were. We thought something happened." The first one beamed, straightening her skirt.

"No, nothing happened. I knew everyone missed my presence, so I opted to stop in," Harmony said, a sarcastic smile gracing her rosebud lips.

"We're glad you stopped in," she said, walking briskly to the other desk as she began typing—a job which Harmony knew was long overdue.

"Did you hear her? She has some nerve. Can't believe she acts like she owns the place." A small grin played on Harmony's lips as she read the Instant Message.

"Anne, you really need to be careful when you gossip. Who knows, you could end up sending the person you slandered an Instant Message about them," Harmony said slowly.

"Oh, no, Harmony. I would never talk about you; that was for someone else we were talking about earlier…before you came."

The elevator door opened a second time, revealing Chardonnay, sipping a large drink from Mcdonald's in her right hand. Harmony always feared that the elevator would collapse—with Chardonnay taking it every day.

"Y'all, the traffic was crazy! I had to take my kids to school," she said, as she attempted to deceive Harmony.

"Hm…really? It didn't seem that bad to me," Harmony said, as she reflected on her drive.

"Yeah, I94 was backed up. Crazy traffic." She ran a hand through her messy blonde lace front.

"I thought your kids went to West Haven?" Harmony's left brow shot up.

"Yeah, they do. They're in district 206; the best in the nation."

"That's too bad, they were late today."

"Nah, my kids know they bet not be late. They walk across the street every morning, faithfully. I don't play," she said with a snug smile, as she greeted Anne with a nod.

"Hm…so you were on I94 this morning because your kids made you late, but your kids walked across the street to school and made it on time? Mmm-hmm," Harmony said, rubbing her chin.

"Girl, you crazy." Chardonnay let out a stiff laugh, realizing her lie was exposed.

"I need to see you two in my office," Juanita walked in and told them sharply, before walking away. Harmony and Chardonnay exchanged thoughtful glances, and then followed her.

∞ ∞ ∞

"What's up?" Chardonnay asked, squeezing herself into Juanita's chair.

"First, y'all can't be coming in here late," Juanita scolded, as she collected a vintage teacup from Chardonnay with a warning glare.

"I know," Harmony replied, without looking up.

"I feel you J, but last night my baby had my legs in the air." Chardonnay raised her hands helplessly.

"Ew." Harmony stuck her finger in her mouth, as if gagging, and scrunched her nose. "TMI, Sis. TMI." She gagged.

"Yuck! That's just…no," Juanita said, disgust evident on her face.

"I don't want to hear about your endeavors. Some things I NEVER want to know, and that is one of them." Harmony continued.

"Y'all crazy." Chardonnay slapped her oversized thighs, in a fit of uncontrollable laughter.

'Well, I brought you in here to tell you to train Harmony… on your position," Juanita said, her expression turning blank.

"What? Why?" Chardonnay suspiciously inquired.

"My boss wants Sales Coordinators, including the temps, cross-trained."

"Well, if they are eliminating positions, why would I need to train her?"

"Just do it. It's an order from upstairs." She shrugged.

"Okay, no problem, J. I'll train her," she said, with a stiff smile.

"Chardonnay, I need to talk to Harmony alone now."

"Okay, cool," she muttered, as she struggled to get out of the chair.

"Harmony, they're getting rid of Chardonnay. You are replacing her," Juanita said, as soon as the door slammed behind Chardonnay.

"What?" Her well-carved brow shot up. "Um, okay," she added, a confused look on her face.

"Make sure you don't tell her," Juanita warned.

"Okay."

"Also, could you do me a favor and pick up my lunch in building C? Thanks, hun."

"Ah…sure," Harmony muttered, getting up from the chair.

∞ ∞ ∞

"I hate this stupid job," Harmony whined, as she slammed the car door shut.

"It's like being in hell. Playing dumb all day…for what? Pennies. I can't live like this. God, I know you got something better for me. Dealing with all these losers who sabotage my work and create chaos because they think I want their job. They can have their jobs! I want millions," she paused, "correction, billions. Ah." She slammed her hand into the steering wheel.

Harmony strapped her seatbelt on, and geared the car into motion. 'This too shall pass.' by India Arie filled the car.

"Thank you, God," she whispered, looking up.

Chapter 3: Just Can't Stay Away

*H*ello, Stranger," the caller chirped, as Harmony put the phone on speaker and placed it on her dresser.

"Funny, it's been years, and you still consider me a stranger. Yet you keep calling?" Harmony said, as she struggled to keep her work bun in place with eco gel.

"You keep answering, so you must miss me."

"Hello?" he asked, when nothing came through.

"Oh, were you talking to me? Figured you were talking to someone in the background." Harmony smirked as she hooked her pearl necklace in place.

"Still the same Harmony." The caller chuckled.

"Kwame, what do you want?" Harmony asked, slightly irritated. She collected the phone from the dresser and placed it on the bed, where she sat to fix her shoe.

Kwame chuckled before saying, "What? I'm just calling to check on you, honest." Harmony could see him raising his hands up and placing them on his chest, as usual.

"Well, since that's all you wanted, I'm fine. Goodbye," she spat and hung up. Satisfied, she bent down properly to lace her shoes and moisturize her feet.

"Not again," Harmony murmured, as she pressed the power button.

"Wait, I know you just didn't hang up. Tell me I dreamt that."

"Next, you'll be asking me to tell you a bedtime story," she scoff and sneered. "Now, what did you really call for?"

"Alright, alright. I need a favor," he said, his voice lower than usual.

"No, you need Jesus so you can get *favor*."

"You are crazy." He laughed. "I probably do, but baby, I need you to help me out."

"What now?" she asked, as she grabbed her purse from the dresser.

"Beautiful, can you go pick up my bag at the airport? I'm traveling, and I can't make it back in time. Baby, it's in my locker, but I just can't get back in time."

"*Bawwwwha*. Do I seem slow to you? You sound like one of them crazy emails, telling me to ship something to Nigeria. Besides, last time I checked; I wasn't a postal worker."

"Alright, dang." His voice came out small, almost like a whisper. "Well, could you at least let me buy you dinner?"

"Now you want to buy me dinner?"

"What? Can't I spend time with an attractive queen?" he teased.

"Go on," Harmony said, a small smile playing on her lips.

"Baby, I got you something." That was exactly what Harmony liked to hear. The smile grew wider, but there was no reflection of it in her voice.

"Okay, what is it?" she asked, sounding bored.

"Meet me at Mr. Chow's at nine tomorrow night. Don't be late. I have a surprise for you."

"Mr. Chow's…. mmh, I love that place," Harmony cooed.

"I know," Kwame said, proud that he had gotten Harmony to eat out of his hand.

"What's the gift?" she asked, the smile widening.

"Baby come find out," Kwame mused.

"At least give me a clue," Harmony whined, rolling her eyes at Kwame's tricks.

"It's shiny," he said under his breath.

"Shiny. Mmh, ok, I'll see you tomorrow."

"Night baby," he said sweetly, before ending the call.

Harmony shoved the phone into her bag, grabbed her car key, and walked out of the room. As she turned the lights off, another call came through.

"Hello?" she asked, a bit cross. The last thing she needed before going to her awful job was a series of annoying calls.

"Hello, this is Detective Holmes, from the Vincent Police Department. May I speak to Harmony Wentworth?" The deep baritone voice filled Harmony's ears, making the hair on her body stand up.

"This is she," she said quickly. She wanted to sound calm, by all means.

"Yes, we have some questions we want to ask you."

"I'm glad you called."

"You are?" the detective asked, his voice laced with curiosity.

"Yes, I would be more than glad to have the idiot thrown in prison for the rest of his life."

"You would?" he asked again. Harmony was a bit taken aback by all his strange questions, but she continued talking, anyway.

"Of course, if there is *anything,* and I do mean *anything,* that I can do, I'll gladly help."

"Well, since you mentioned it…would you mind coming down to the station to give a statement?"

"With pleasure," she chirped. A part of her was happy she had the opportunity of meeting the man behind the voice, but the bigger part wanted to see Ronnie behind bars. "Are you still located off 5th Street?"

"Yes."

"I'll be there in 15 minutes," she said, and hung up.

∞ ∞ ∞

"Hello, I'm Harmony Wentworth. Detective Holmes is expecting me," Harmony said, as she walked up to the officers at the desk.

"Ms. Wentworth. Come in, have a seat." The detective led her to his private office.

"I'm so glad you called; that guy should have been locked up years ago," she said, studying the detective's features. His physical appearance certainly went well with his face. He had a broad chest that was covered in a black fitted shirt.

"Well, let's get down to business." He ran a large hand on his jaw; it looked like it was chipped from granite.

"With pleasure," she said, with a small smile.

"We see here that you've been in contact with Kwame."

"What?" Harmony chocked out, a small cough following suit.

"Ma'am, we have reasons to believe that you have been in contact with Kwame." He leaned back into his chair.

"What's this about?" Harmony broke her eye contact with him; instead, she focused her attention on a trophy case behind him.

"Have you heard from him?" he asked, as he leaned in to study her demeanor.

"I thought I was here to speak about being attacked by Ronnie." She shifted her gaze back to the detective.

"Who?" He raised his left brow.

"You know, the man that tried to murder my family. I mean, you bring me in here to ask me about a rapper from the '80s who wore polka-a-dots? Granted, I am a fashion expert, but really?" She raised her hands in mock disbelief, tearing her gaze away from the detective.

"No, ma'am, not the rapper Kwame. Kwame LaRue, your ex," he said, a grin plastered on his face. Harmony felt like lying him down on his table and wiping the grin off of him.

"Ahhh…ex? Look, I am a very busy woman. I would appreciate it if you got to the point."

"We need to speak with Kwame. We have some questions we need to ask him. So, I ask you again…Have you been in contact with him?"

"I haven't talked to anyone, yet," she whispered the last part under her breath, causing the detective to shoot her a curious look.

"Detective, if this is not going to be about Ronnie, then our conversation is over." She slammed her hands lightly on the table, picked her purse up, and moved out of the chair.

"Ms. Wentworth, we will be in touch." The detective extended his hands, but Harmony dismissed him.

"Not if I can help it," she whispered, as she walked out.

∞ ∞ ∞

"No, this sorry piece of nothing did not get me caught up in some bull," she said, as she dumped her bag on the passenger's seat and dialed Kwame's number.

"Hello," he said, his voice high pitched and bubbly.

"Hello, is there something you forgot to mention?"

"What?" he asked, sounding genuinely curious.

"So, you're wanted?"

"Wanted? What are you talking about?" His voice went up several octaves.

"You know damn well what I'm talking about. The police just had me at the station. Guess your "shiny" gift was them platinum bracelets," she snarled, as she strapped her seatbelt on.

"What did you tell them?"

Harmony could sense him trying to not sound anxious. "You know… I can't talk to you right now. These lines aren't clear."

"What? Hello? No, this bastard didn't hang up on me," Harmony yelled, tossing the cellphone in the passenger seat.

∞ ∞ ∞

"You two better hurry up! If you miss that bus, you're walking," Joy yelled for the kids, as she unwrapped her charcoal black hair.

"I'm ready," Misa said, as she strolled into the kitchen

"I'm rrrr-ready, too." Miles grabbed his lunch bag off the counter and scurried out of the kitchen with Misa.

Joy sucked her teeth at their childish antics. After successfully getting her hair unwrapped, she moved to the counter and started cleaning up.

"I will be glad when they get out of my house. I have to do *everything!* Shoot, they ought to be grateful!" she complained, as she made purposeful swipes on the messy counter with a dish cloth.

"I know this girl didn't. See, that's what I'm talking about. I told them good last night, make sure they had everything. Now, I gotta go all out of *my* way to bring her, *her* lunch. This girl." She face palmed as she saw Misa's pink lunch bag on the kitchen counter.

∞ ∞ ∞

Joy walked into the front office at Misa's school, sweating profusely, with Misa's bag in hand. She swiped a napkin over her face as she approached the curvy brunette.

"Hello, my child forgot her lunch," she said, as she stretched the bag towards the secretary.

"Who's your child?" she asked, adjusting her glasses.

"Misa. That's M-I-S-"

"Oh, I know Misa. How's she doing?" she asked, with a big smile.

"She's okay, I guess," Joy said, a bit puzzled.

"You said you're bringing her lunch?" She scrunched unkept carved brows a little as she searched her computer.

"Yes," Joy said, getting a bit impatient.

"Well, it shows here she's out today."

"What? Who approved that?" Joy asked, dropping the lunch bag on the table.

"Mmh," She looked through the computer again. "You did, when you called this morning."

"Oh, that's right," she said, her eyes darting left and right. "My mistake, no wonder she didn't grab her lunch. Duh, I just saw it on the counter," she quickly added with a clumsy smile.

"Oh, it's okay, happens all the time," the secretary replied, equally returning the smile.

"Well, I'll just take this with me; you have a blessed day." She smiled again and started walking out.

"You too. Tell Misa to feel better," she called after Joy.

"Will do," she said over her shoulder.

∞ ∞ ∞

"I know this brat did not have the nerve to call herself off. When I see her, Lord keep me," she muttered to herself, as she strapped her seatbelt on. She was about to kick the car into motion, when the sound of her phone interrupted.

"Hey, Joy, what's up?"

"Peace, do you know what this demon brat just did?" She paused, turned the car on, and connected the bluetooth. "That heifer had the nerve to call herself out of school. After everything I do for her and her brother, she had the nerve to try an embarrass me."

"She did what?"

"Yes, Misa. When I see her, I'm *gon'* catch a case." Joy fumed, as she took a sharp turn.

Peace's laughter filled the car, causing Joy to roll her eyes. "Joy, don't beat her. Besides, I can't come to get you if you get locked up. I don't get paid until next week." She laughed again. Joy glared at the phone, like Peace could see her.

"I got $100 to get out." She took another sharp, angry turn.

"No, it's not worth it. Just put her in time out." Joy could see the images of Peace laughing and throwing her head back. She wanted to gouge her eyes out, along with Misa's.

"Time out?" Joy let out a dry laugh. "That girl is a teenager, how about times up? It hurts!" she whined.

Love, Peace, Joy and... Harmony

"I go to work each day to make money to help *them*, so *they* can eat, because they own mama didn't want to be bothered. I give those kids my last, and all I ask them to do is go to school, clean up at home, and go to church. Everything I ask them to do is for *their* benefit. By going to school, they will be able to get a decent job. By cleaning up they can live in a clean house, and by going to church, both will learn about God so they can navigate this world. But no, all they do is sneak and do me dirty," she rambled, while Peace waited patiently for her to finish.

"Studies show communication is key to dealing with teenagers. Joy, they might not understand now, but one day they will realize all you do for them," she reassured her, as she tried to not burst into laughter again. Joy would definitely take her head off.

"*Hemp*, they better. I gave up my life for them. You know, I think I know where she is. She's been hanging with this fast-tail girl lately. I bet she's with her. I'm going to go look for her. I'll call you later."

"Okay, be careful," Peace said with a sigh.

"I will."

∞ ∞ ∞

"Misa, isn't this great? Look at how cute I look." Peyton, Misa's friend, twirled in front of a mirror at Forever 16, a store in the city's mall.

"Is that all you can think about? We are so in trouble if we get caught," Misa said, as she scanned the boutique for familiar faces.

"Relax," Peyton said, as she stepped into the light, her strawberry blonde hair shining brightly. "We're not going to get caught, I told you. My parents are out of town." She did another twirl.

"Well, Peyton, mine isn't. I can't believe I let you talk me into calling in. If Joy finds out…" she trailed off. She couldn't even imagine what Joy would do if she caught her.

"She's not going to find out, I love these jeans. I'm so getting them." She twirled again, her curls bouncing behind her, as she strolled into the dressing room.

"Come on, let's go." She grabbed Misa's hand and started walking out of the store.

"Peyton, the register is that way," Misa whined, pointing at the front counter.

"Shh… you'll blow my cover," she said, plastering a smile on her face.

"What? I hope you're not doing what I think you're doing?" Misa gasped as they approached the security area.

"Relax, security is watching. Act natural." Peyton threw a nice smile at a guard, before pushing Misa forward.

∞ ∞ ∞

"Do these jeans make my butt look bigger?" She turned to Misa, a wide smile on her face.

"I can't believe you did that," Misa said, as she sat down on Peyton's messy bed.

"Did what?" she asked in a high-pitched tone, shrugging.

"Stole," Misa said, without looking up.

"Relax, it's not stealing. It's kind-of-like modeling," she said and did another twirl.

"Modeling?"

"You see," Peyton began, "if anyone asks where I brought my jeans from, I tell them the store. If anything, I should be getting paid for wearing their clothes."

"You're crazy," Misa chastised. "Just remember, when you are getting more clothes for your 'modeling', not to have me with you. I am not going to jail."

"Whatever... Scary-Sherry. The guys should be here any second. Remember, we're eighteen, so don't be immature." She giggled.

The doorbell rang, causing Misa to jump up. "They're here," Peyton said, pushing her cleavage up.

"Hey, Sexy," Jax cooed, as he stepped into the house.

"Hi, Jax." Peyton giggled at the sight of the two messy haired teenage boys

"This is my guy, K. J." Jax pointed at the bigger of the pair, who waved in response.

"Sup." K.J. clasped his gloved hand in to Peyton's who giggled again.

"This is my best friend, Misa." Peyton gestured towards Misa, but she was having none of it.

"Hi," she greeted, a permanent scowl plastered on her face.

"Well, we will leave you two to talk. Jax, let me show you my room," Peyton said, grabbing Jax's hand.

"Peyton?" Misa questioned through her teeth, her eyebrows going up. "I know you're not leaving me with him."

"Relax, Misa. I'll be upstairs; I kind of have something 'private' to tell Jax." She laughed, taking his hands in hers again and intertwining their fingers.

"It's cool, she can watch. I'm not shy," Jax said, a smug smile playing on his chapped lips.

"Ew, I'll be in the bathroom," Misa excused herself, while Peyton and Jax headed upstairs to her room.

After several rings of the doorbell, K.J. opened the door.

Joy ran in, immediately. "Where is she?"

"Where is who?" he asked, sounding bored.

"Don't give me that boy, my thirteen-year-old, I'm going to kill." Joy walked to the living room, her giant steps making quiet thuds.

"Thirteen? I didn't do anything. I didn't know they were thirteen. My momma *gon'* kill me." He mumbled the last part. He turned his hat around and straightened his clothes, fear evident in his eyes.

"Tell that to the judge, Pedo. Misa, I know you're in here. You better come out, *now!*" she yelled, pacing back and forth.

"Hey Joy." She walked into living room, her knees shaking.

"Don't give me that, you fast-good-for-nothing tramp. Wait till we get home. You *gon'* be on lockdown. Get in the car, *now!*" Misa scurried past Joy quickly.

"What's all the yelling about?" Peyton asked, as she descended the stairs.

"And *you*, you scandalous thing. You stay away from Misa. Your momma and daddy ought to be ashamed."

In all the scolding, Jax walked downstairs confidently.

"Oh...sh--"

"Thirteen years old, skipping school, to lay with a grown man. Your momma gonna hear about this."

"Ms. Joy, I'm sorry," Peyton said, bowing her head down in shame. Her voice came out really small; Joy had to strain her ears to listen. "Don't tell my mom. Nothing happened."

"I'm not *gon'* tell her...you are." Joy dialed Peyton's mom's number with a smirk and placed the call on speaker. "Start talking,"

"Um, hello, Mom. Um, Ms. Joy is here at the house."

"Tell her what you did."

"Misa and I skipped. Jax and K.J. came over, but nothing happened, Mom, I swear."

"*What?* Get *those* people out of my house, *now!*" she bellowed.

"My mom says you have to leave." Peyton pointed at the door, her hands shaking.

"Hemp. Serves y'all right. Get out right now!" she yelled, making the boys run out of the house. She then turned and faced Peyton again. "Just don't make no sense."

"Um, Ms. Joy, she means you, too," Peyton said, scratching behind her ears.

Joy became heated when she realized the mother was not as accepting of her as she thought. She rolled her eyes in anger, and then shot Peyton a final warning glare as she powered off the phone.

∞ ∞ ∞

"I hate this job. Lord, I know you got something better. This isn't it for me," Harmony whined, as she typed away on her computer.

"Harmony, have you done the annual report on the Western Accounts?" Juanita's voluptuous figure strolled into Harmony's workspace casually, with a straight face.

"Western Accounts?" Harmony slowly dragged her head up from her former focus.

"Chardonnay's accounts, the ones I told you to take over."

"No, Chardonnay only showed me Eastern Accounts. She never mentioned anything about Western Accounts." Harmony shrugged.

"I need both of you in my office, *now!*"

"J, I told her to do them," Chardonnay said quickly, as they walked into the office.

"No, you didn't. Chardonnay," Harmony tighten her upper lip, "you never mentioned anything about it."

"Yeah, I did." She pointed an accusing finger at Harmony. "J, you know I love my job, I wouldn't mess up anything so important. If it weren't for this job, I wouldn't be able to feed my kids. You know I live for Cashmere and Cynnamon," she said, facing Juanita.

"What I *know*, is that you *never* mentioned it."

"Well, I don't know who's lying, but someone is going to--"

"What do you mean, you don't know who's lying?" Harmony cut Juanita short. "Why would I lie? This job doesn't pay me enough to lie. I am not some bottom-barreled person who cannot get another job. I have an associate's, bachelors, and master's degree. Yet, I'm settling for drama for less than 40,000 a year? Like I said, I don't have to lie." She rolled her eyes and straightened her skirt.

"Ooh see, J, I told you she has an attitude. She thinks she's better than everybody."

"I don't think, I know," she yelled. "I'm Harmony Wentworth. If it weren't for this job, I would never speak to you. If it weren't for my taxes, your brats wouldn't eat. You're lazy, fake, and phony. You don't give a damn about your kids." She fumed, pacing back and forth in Juanita's office.

"Harmony?" Juanita cautioned.

"You're too busy whoring around, trying to get some bum to lift your fat rolls and give you some." She pointed at Chardonnay. "You should be ashamed."

"Harmony!" Juanita slammed her fist into the table. "You're fired!" she yelled, gesturing towards the door.

"You and this fat bear can kiss what I twist, and I don't mean my wrist," she retorted, as she strolled confidently out of the office.

Chapter 4: Everybody Gets Tired

*J*oy, are you ready?" Peace asked, as she checked her make-up in front of Joy's mirror.

"Calm down, I had to ensure the kids were down the street." She smoothened the edge of her hair. "Can't trust them."

"Have you talked to Harmony?" she asked, as she applied lip-gloss. Peace scrunched her nose.

"No, I haven't talked to Ms. Can't Keep A Job," she mocked.

"I know." Peace sighed. "We went over the psychology behind job loss in class last week; it's so sad that she was fired again."

"It ain't sad. If she learned how to keep her mouth closed, she'd be fine. Harmony goes into a company and tries to take over; people don't like that." She shrugged, grabbing her purse.

"Joy, could you get her a job with you?" Peace asked, hopefully.

"She already worked with me, only lasted a month." Peace threw her hands over her mouth to keep herself from bursting into an uncontrollable fit of laughter. She stared at Peace for a while, wondering if they came from the same roots. Her beaming green eyes and curly brown hair tumbled down her shoulders beautifully, with her pouty lips glistening under the sunlight.

"Right, I forgot about that. Let's take your car," she said, grabbing Joy's keys.

"Let me guess…no gas?" Joy said, with a raised eyebrow.

"Sis, why would you say that? Maybe I just want to ride in comfort, because I know your superior driving skills assure my safety," she said playfully, as they turned the lights off.

"Bahahaha… who are you trying to fool?" Joy messed Peace's hair up a bit, causing her to flinch.

"Yeah, I don't have gas," she muttered, and they both burst into laughter.

∞ ∞ ∞

"Hello," Harmony said, sounding gloomy. Her voice came out frustrated and sad.

"Hello, Stranger."

"Stranger nothing, what do you want Kwame?" She adjusted her blanket.

"I was in your area. I wanted to apologize. I have something for you."

"Keep it." She crossed her arms.

"Harmony, for such a pretty woman, you sure can be mean."

"Who's at my door?" she whined, when the rambunctious sound of someone knocking filled her living room.

She removed her blanket, placed her juice on the table, and walked solemnly to the door; a permanent scowl on her face.

She opened the door slowly, revealing Kwame, his freshly tighten dreads pulled back, with a bouquet of roses in his left hand, and champagne in the other. Harmony's scowl deepened, considering the fact that she despised both of the gifts.

"Opportunity just knocked," he said with a smile.

"Guess you never heard closed doors can't be open?" she retorted, with an eye roll. She was about to add something, but the muffled *ding* of her oven timer sounded, and she turned away.

Kwame took a seat on the sofa Harmony was previously occupying, as he scanned the room casually. The lavish decor intrigued him, as he smiled at a picture of Harmony on her fifth birthday.

"Cooking me dinner? I'm flattered," he said, with a smug smile.

"More like delusional," she said, as she took a seat, stuffing a piece of chocolate into her mouth. "Why are you really here?"

"To apologize. Baby, I messed up."

"You did."

"I cleared the situation up," he said, grabbing a glass. "I'm a changed man." He poured himself a drink and lifted it up. "Cheers! To new beginnings."

"Hate to ruin your "I Have a Dream" speech, but I have an appointment I'm late for; let yourself out."

"Oh, sorry, I just remembered I have to be somewhere, too." He stood up quickly and dropped the glass. "I am headed to Kingston, Jamaica; good seeing you." He smiled and headed for the door.

"Wish I could say the same."

∞ ∞ ∞

"Hello?" Misa looked through the window to check if the women were really gone. Ever since the incident at Peyton's, Joy employed one of the strictest babysitters in town to keep watch over Misa and Miles while she was out. She made sure to drop them off and get them herself.

"Hey Peyton, it's me." Misa said, her eyes darting back and forth.

"Whose number is this?"

"This lady's house; Joy made us come."

"Don't tell me… you're at the babysitter's again?" She started laughing.

"Whatever. It's your fault, you know. I can't even use my cell because of you."

"I did you a favor." Peyton laughed. "That thing was hideous; you didn't even have internet. It always dropped calls." The duo burst into laughter.

"Anyways…"

"Well…I'm late…" she trailed off.

"Late for what?"

"You know," Peyton trailed off again. "I'm *late*. Do I have to spell it out? My monthly visitor did not make a house call this month." She burst into laughter, taking Misa aback.

"What?" Misa's mouth hung open. "Wait…do you mean you're pregnant?" she whispered.

"I don't know for sure. I have a test I bought, but I've been too scared to take it."

"Oh my…by who?" She gasped again. She couldn't wrap her head around it yet.

"Gee, thanks." Misa could taste Peyton rolling her eyes.

"I'm just saying, do you know who the father is?"

"Are you calling me a *thot?* I mean, of course, I know. It's…well, it's got to be. No, wait…well, who cares about that. If I am, I'm not keeping it. My mother will pay to get it fixed."

"Girl, aren't you scared? You can't kill a baby," Misa whispered, again.

"I'm not. It's not a baby, it's barely anything."

"Huh? Who told you that? It is a real baby."

"I am not being a Baby's Momma, not in this world. My mom would die."

"If you talk to her, she will be mad but probably accept it."

"She didn't accept it before."

"This isn't the first time?" Misa's eyes widened in horror as she covered her mouth to keep herself from gasping loudly.

"That was last year. I don't care about that; I didn't even like the boy. I need somewhere to take the test. Who's at your house?"

"Nobody, I'm down the street."

"Meet me at your house, ASAP."

"Heck no! That's how I got grounded… listening to you." She thought about what Joy would do if she caught her. She would definitely place her on a chopping board and cook her for dinner.

"Come on, you're my best friend. I need you," Peyton pleaded in her most annoying whine.

"Okay, I'm on my way." She gave in and ended the call.

∞ ∞ ∞

"Anybody home?" Harmony called, as she walked into Joy's, after letting herself in with her key.

"Did you hear something?" Misa whispered, looking out her door.

"No, scary," she muttered, without taking her eyes off the cylindrical pregnancy test tube. She was pacing back and forth.

"Someone's here." Misa's eyes widened at the sound of the ice machine. She peeped out the door again, but saw no one. "Joy's going to kill me," she whispered, gesturing for Peyton to hide the test.

"Ooh…you're in trouble now."

"I knew I shouldn't have listened to you."

"How can we get out without getting caught?"

"Let's just hide." Misa grabbed Peyton's hand and led her into her closet.

"I can't believe that fast heifer had the nerve to leave from down the street." Joy stormed into the house, with beads of sweat on her forehead.

"Joy, what are you fussing about now?" Harmony took a sip of water and adjusted her hair in the mirror.

"Misa, that ungrateful thing," she said, through her teeth.

"What'd she do now? Let me guess, she ran away from your crazy butt." Harmony burst into laughter.

"No, Harm this is serious, she left. Joy and I rode around the neighborhood looking for her. We talked about missing children in psychology a few months ago." Peace informed Harmony, as she walked into the living room.

"Misa is probably with that little skank she always with." Joy fussed, as she put the groceries away.

"Did you try calling her?" Harmony asked.

"No," she said, as she shoved the canned goods into place. "Miles, go upstairs till I call you," she instructed, without looking up.

"To think I go out of my way to take care of these kids. Own momma didn't want them. They're so ungrateful. I'm trying to cook a surprise dinner for Miles, and this little thing trying to ruin it. She's not going to ruin my day," she said, as she struggled to gather the cans of peas that fell during her rambling.

"We know, Joy. You took the kids in," Harmony said. She bent to help Joy pick the scattered groceries up. "You remind the family every day. It's not like you're not getting benefits for having them. Remember…YOU CHOSE to take them."

"You're not *gon'* come in my house and disrespect me; you didn't step up."

"You two, please. Miles is upstairs," Peace cautioned.

"Joy, stop acting like you don't get benefits for them. Hell, tell the truth. You stole them from their momma. You and Giovanni's thieving momma did the bogus paperwork," she yelled.

"Shut up! Harmony, you don't know *everything!*"Joy faced both Harmony and Peace.

"Both of you stop, this is not the time. We need to find Misa."

"I don't care if she doesn't come back. She acts just like Harmony. A smart-mouth-mess." She raised her hands and walked to the fridge.

"Better to have a smart mouth, than a dumb mind," Harmony retorted.

"Y'all, stop!" Peace got in between both of them. "It's Miles's day. We're better than this; look up."

"What?"

"Huh?"

"Look up." Both women looked up. "God does not want you to do that," she pleaded. Harmony and Joy stole glances at each other, then mumble apologies under their breath.

"Whh-whha... What's this?" Miles pointed the tube at the three sisters.

"What in the..." Joy gasped, her mouth hanging open. "Give me that, and go back upstairs until I call you." She collected it and faced both Peace and Harmony. "Which one of you pregnant?"

"Don't look at me." Harmony raised her hands up and looked at Peace.

"Don't look at me, either."

"I just cleaned the bathroom today; I would have seen it. Wait, someone else is in this house. " She handed Peace the tube and ran upstairs. For a big person, Peace wondered how she moved so quickly.

"You no good heathen." Joy's heart went on overdrive, as she opened the closet and found the girls. Without thinking twice, she launched at Misa, but

Peace and Harmony jumped in. Taking their cue, the girls scurried down-stairs, with Joy following suit. "It's not me, Don't--"

"It's mine, Ms. Joy," Peyton interrupted, "but it's a false alarm."

"You demon from hell, get out of my house, right now," Joy barked. Without looking back, Peyton bolted out of the house, leaving the door open.

"Joy, calm down. Don't do nothing you *gon'* regret." Harmony moved closer to her and placed a hand on her shoulders.

"Yeah, Joy, remember, I can't come to get you if you get locked up. You know I don't get paid until next week." Peace tried to inject some humor, but Joy was having none of it.

"I don't care, I'll do time to get away from this brat."

"Hey, family." L walked in, a wide smile on his face.

"Family my…" Joy trailed off. "You know what, since you always defending her, you take her," she said, facing Harmony.

"Like hell." Harmony moved back. "I don't do the kid thing."

"If you didn't want us, why did you take us, then?" Misa covered her eyes with her hands to try to keep the tears from falling.

"Who you think you talking to?" Joy faced the crying child and chastised.

"Chill, Joy." Harmony shot her a warning glare, then faced Misa. "Misa, it's not that I don't want to take you, I just don't have any certificates. I'm not qualified to raise no babies."

"What's going on?" L moved closer.

"If she doesn't take her," Joy warned, as she took a seat, "I'm *gon'* kill her. I'm tired, and I need a break. Ungrateful brat," she spat, eyeing Misa.

"Fine, Misa, get an overnight bag. You can come sleepover until Joy re-gains her senses," Harmony said, with a warm smile.

"No, I'm *done*! Take him, too!" She gestured towards Miles.

"Wait, I can't do both."

"Joy, I'll take him." Peace drew Miles closer and led him upstairs.

"All y'all, get out. *Now!*" They all scurried and left.

"I'm spending the night with you, Sis," L said, as he turned around.

Chapter 5: A Piece of Man

$\mathcal{B}$lessings, this is Joy," Joy said calmly.

"Blessings?" Ronnie tried to suppress his laughter. "When you start that?"

"Oh, Ronnie. Hey. Okay, bye." She smacked her lips.

"Who are you saying bye to?"

"That's just my brother—L— leaving."

"Better be just L," he spat. "That's all I get, just a *hey.* You don't love me no more?"

"Mmh," Joy knew Ronnie too well, nothing passed that phone call.

"It's an *Mmh* now? Now you got to think about it huh? Your nosy sisters, they got in your head."

"Don't talk about my family," she hissed.

"I'll talk about…you know," he started, his voice decreasing. "I was calling you to bless you, but maybe I'll call somebody else."

"What?" she asked. She tried desperately to keep the anxiety from being evident in her voice.

"You are always talking about being able to give to the church and all. Well, I got this cleaning service. I'm going to let you invest in it. I only trust you, cause you my rider."

"Your what?"

"My Rider. Dang girl, you need to get out more. My Rider, it's a new song by XL."

"Oh, Harmony's friend." Joy shrugged.

"So, what's up? You in or what?" Ronnie asked.

"How much do I need to invest?" Joy knew Ronnie, anything involving money, meant she had to be the one doing the most.

"Just meet me at the Title Store. I'll do the rest." He beamed, happy to have Joy wrapped around his finger.

"Title Store?" Joy paused, confused. "Why are we going there?"

"Man, damn, listen. How else we gon' get on. Just meet me on 125th."

"Ronnie, I'm not going back out there," she said.

"Oh, now you not coming. You didn't have no problem coming out here to lay with me. I should call your Bishop. Let him know his secretary ain't living right." Ronnie knew that the best way to get Joy to succumb was through subtle threats.

"Whatever, Ronnie." Joy tapped her foot. She had gotten tired of Ronnie and his blackmail.

"Look, I didn't want to say nothing, but I was gon' take you to look for a ring," he said slowly.

"I'm on my way," Joy chirped, and ended the call—clapping her hands together.

She didn't need Ronnie to see it, but the excitement was seeping through her as she dialed Peace's number. Her smile spread widely as she tapped her left foot anxiously, while waiting for Peace to answer the call.

"Hey, Sis. I'm Glad you're feeling better. You know, Joy, we held mock counseling sessions last semester. I can offer a weekly meeting," Peace said sweetly.

"No! Guess what?" she said, her voice high pitched, as she downed a glass of water.

"Ronnie just proposed!" she yelled, without allowing Peace to try at guessing. "He's starting a cleaning service, and we're going to look for rings. My prayers have been answered," she shouted again, her hands going over her mouth in excitement.

"Are you serious?" Peace asked flatly.

"Yes, I'm serious. Whatever you do… don't tell Harmony." She sucked her teeth.

"Why?"

"Because she doesn't want me to be happy."

"Okay," she said, her voice sounding bored and uninterested.

"How Miles doing?"

"He's doing good."

"I know he is probably a lot of work?"

"No, he's cool."

"I know you want him to come home. Now you see how much I do."

"I'm spectacular, Miles doesn't bother me."

"Well, since they are my responsibility…I don't feel right just leaving them with you guys," Joy said, her face falling. "I know you and Harmony have your own lives. I know y'all don't know anything about raising children."

"Joy, you must want them to come home." Peace's laughter filled Joy's ears, making her smile. "I knew you'd miss them. I'll drop him off later."

"Well," she whispered, pumping her fists in the air, "if you want to. Have you spoken to Harmony?"

"Yeah, she's got Misa waiting on her hand and foot, you know Harmony."

"Misa is probably dying to get home." Joy threw her head back and laughed. "You can tell Harmony to drop her off too."

"Tell her yourself, she just walked up."

"Hello," Harmony said, sounding like she'd rather be doing anything in the world than having that phone call.

"Agh, Harmony," Joy said, unsure of the tone to use.

"I know you missed me. Must be awful to have to deal with yourself without having me in your life."

"You really are sick," Joy mocked.

"Of haters." Harmony let out a small, self-important laugh. "But other than that, I'm well. I have a fabulous life, you know."

"Well… I'm getting married," Joy said softly, unable to hide the excitement in her voice.

"To what?"

"Ronnie and I are going to look at rings today, we are starting a cleaning service." Joy clapped her hands happily.

"He can start with himself," Harmony Jeered. "Tell him to do society a favor, find a bridge and lean forward."

"That's evil." Joy gasped.

"No, that's going green. Ridding the world of unnecessary trash."

"Since you can't be happy for me, I might just elope."

"Why not wait until he goes back to jail? They'll marry you for free," Harmony mocked and hung up.

"Stupid," Joy muttered under her breath, as she dialed the number again.

"Hello."

"Where is she?" Joy said sharply, not bothering to greet Peace.

"Who?"

"That evil witch you call your sister." Joy sneered.

"Harmony, Joy wants you," Peace called out.

"Tell her I'm not taking any more calls." She paused. "On second thought, tell her to have her people call my people, and we can do lunch. Ciao."

"Her people." Joy let out a stiff laughter. "Only people she got is unemployment. Tell that want-to-be diva to get a job or better yet get a man— cause Joy Wentworth already got one!" she yelled and turned the phone off.

∞ ∞ ∞

"Who does that fat Jezebel think she is?" Harmony fumed, as she walked into her home. Just because I don't sleep with everything at the church picnic, does not mean I cannot get a man. I am Harmony Wentworth. I am worth the wait," she vented, picking her phone up.

"Hello?"

"Hello, may I speak to Harmony." The voice sounded familiar, but Harmony couldn't place a finger on it.

"Speaking, and you are?"

"You forgot about me already?" the caller stifled an awkward laugh.

"Yo, this is Tore," he chirped, hoping she would remember. "You gave me Platinum's number— we did an event."

"Oh, and you're calling me because…"

Tore let out another laugh. "I wanted to say thank you."

"You're welcome, Good day," Harmony said stiffly and removed the phone from her ear.

"You wildlin. Wait, don't hang up. I wanted to send you a thank you gift."

"Did you, now?" she mused, a smile playing on her lips.

"How does a trip to NY sound?" he asked, hopefully.

"Silent. Now if you said Paris, I might have heard you."

"You are hilarious. No seriously, I want to fly you out for dinner. Yo, my treat."

"I Guess you never heard of Stranger Danger? You will never kill me for my skin. I saw 'Silence of the Lambs'. I also know Jeffery Dahmer and John Wayne Gacy got copycats. You will never get me."

"You are a funny lady." Tore burst into a hysterical laugh. "I just want to thank you."

"And people in Hell want ice water. Good day," she said flatly and turned the phone off.

Parched, Harmony went into the kitchen to grab an orange drink. She emptied the content into a glass tumbler, and settled down in a chair, while she checked her phone.

'Text from Tore popped on her notification screen.

Tore: *Yo, not to bother you, just wanted to put a face behind that beautiful voice. There's a ticket waiting at the airport with your name on it. It includes a shopping spree.*

Harmony: *If you text me again, I'm going to text you Cash Money style.*

Tore: *What?*

Harmony: *Since you don't listen…My block hot, my block burn, my block on fire, and I blocked you and yours. Oh, and if that doesn't work, try joining that group…what's that group's name? Oh yeah, that's right… New Kids on the… BLOCK!*

Harmony murmured and slammed the phone on the table. In less than two seconds, she got a text notification from an unknown number.

Unknown Number: *Yo, that was cute, but real mental, have more than one line. :) All jokes aside, can I call you?*

Harmony: *You must like abuse? I'm not into S & M.*

Tore: *LOL. So, can I please call you?*

Harmony: *Fine, call.*

Harmony sighed and texted back.

Chapter 6: What You Watching?

"Hey, Sis." L walked into the kitchen, a wide smile on his lips, ready for movie night. Family movie night was a time every member looked forward to. Joy started the tradition about five years back, hoping to draw everyone closer and spend quality time together.

"What did you cook?" he asked, his eyes darting left and right.

"Hey, to you too, L. It's on the stove." She gestured. Joy moved from turning a batter-like substance and walked to check the deep fryer.

"Excuse me, L, you forgot to tell your favorite sister hello." Harmony waved at L.

"Harm, I was just thinking the same thing," Peace added.

"He didn't forget, Peace. Your favorite sister says, thank you,'" Joy said with a smug smile, as she plopped some chicken into her mouth.

"Joy, thank you, but I can speak for myself." Harmony checked her nails smugly and laughed, causing Joy to shoot her an infamous deadly glare.

"Which one of my favorite sisters is going to get me tickets to the Allstar game?" L asked, laughter bubbling in his throat.

"Joy, *you* heard *yo'* brother." Harmony burst into laughter.

"It's like that, huh?" He joined Harmony.

"Man, L, get your floaters to get you tickets," Ken, L's friend, said.

"Floaters?" Peace turned to look at Ken. "Our brother doesn't date floaters."

"Tell em, L," Ken said, as he took a bite of an apple. "You keep five on deck," he added.

"Yo, chill." L moved back, as he caught his sisters' evil glares.

"Don't bring that foolishness in my house. This is the house of the Lord," Joy warned, as she set the chicken on the table.

"You don't have to tell him nothing, Joy. If he keeps talking, I'm *gon'* show him." Harmony pointed at Ken.

"Ken, I know my sister. If I were you, I would bite my tongue," L said, with a slight chuckle.

"That's why I date Becky's."

"Oh…" L's eyes widened at Ken's statement.

"Becky can have you. If she's dumb enough to date a broke man with no home training, that's her stupidity. Ain't no way in the H-E-double-hockey stick, I would leave Bill from a gated community, to go get Bilal from lock-up." Harmony fumed, moving closer to Ken with each word.

"As for me," she continued, "I don't want to adopt a child from Africa or China, and I damn sho don't want to adopt a broke man from America. He is not a child, my truck is not a toy, and it doesn't run for free. You got to have funds to fuel it, and it only takes premium."

"That's why you ain't got a man now," Ken muttered, under his breath.

"Ken, chill, don't say nothing to her." L restrained him.

"When you become a man, then you can speak about grown folks' topics. You are nothing more than an oversized six-year-old," Harmony spat, looking Ken square in the face.

"Okay, y'all chill." L moved in between them.

"I am. He's walking around with all his equity on his back, talking crazy. All he got is a pair of shoes that some woman bought. Shopping at discount stores, buying clothes from ten seasons ago. Thinking he's a baller. You're not a baller. You are a bum. And, FYI, the next time you receive a $150 donation for a pair of shoes, you should invest in a $4 belt. Cause don't nobody want to see your dirty boxers." Harmony brushed L aside and moved closer to Ken.

"Yo, L, get *cho'* sister." He begged.

"Man let's go. She will put hands on you." L pushed him back.

Chapter 7: Grab it Before It's... GONE

Thank you, Lord! Finally got an interview," Harmony said excitedly, as she answered the phone.

"Hey! I just wanted to wish you good luck today,"

"Aw Peace... thanks, Sis." Harmony applied lip gloss. "Can't believe it's on a Saturday," she said, as she fixed her earrings.

"I know, that's so weird. Oh... and Joy asked if you could stop by."

"What does she want now?"

"*Nah*, she doesn't want anything. I think she has money for you."

"What? I didn't say I needed money," Harmony said, a bit cross.

"Yeah, but she said since you ain't working..." Peace trailed off.

"You know, she has that bad being in folk's business...where did you say she left the money at again?" Harmony burst into laughter and Peace joined.

"On the counter in the kitchen," she said, in between laughs.

"Okay, talk to you later."

"K, bye."

∞ ∞ ∞

"Hey beautiful!" Harmony greeted Misa with a big smile, as she strolled into the living room. She loved the role of the cool aunt.

"Harmony!" Misa's big eyes brightened, as she grabbed her favorite aunt into a big hug. Misa intertwined their fingers and led her into the kitchen.

"What did you make?" she asked, her voice bubbling with excitement, as she reached for a cookie.

"No." She gasped. "Joy said not to eat them."

"Well, Misa, Joy's not here." She threw the cookie into her mouth. "These are good, really chocolaty." Harmony licked her fingers.

"Joy said they are for Miles." she quickly arranged the cookies.

"Well, alrighty, then." She laughed and grabbed the envelope from the counter. "Tell her I stopped by, and thanks."

"Okay," Misa said, with a smile.

∞ ∞ ∞

Harmony walked into the restaurant, with her head held high, ready to face the interviewer and get a job.

She located Mr. Schultz and his assistant, sitting at table one; the designated meeting point.

"Hello, Ms. Wentworth?"

"Hello," Harmony said, with a small smile. She didn't want to do too much.

"Did you find us okay?"

"Yes," she muttered, as she took a seat.

"Great, Let's eat. I'm starved." He nodded and signaled for the waiter.

"Well, Ms. Wentworth, I'll just tell you, we were very impressed with your skills," Schultzer said, with a smile.

"Honestly, we do not see skills like these often." His assistant chipped in, adjusting his square frames.

"Thank you." Harmony tried to throw them one of her smiles, but was interrupted by the twist in her stomach. She grabbed on to it slightly, to reduce the pain.

"Can you elaborate on your marketing experience?"

"With pleasure." Harmony smiled, ready to wow them. "Marketing," she paused, to adjust herself in her seat and felt the twist becoming strong knots, "is dear to my heart. I can market any item. My portfolio, mmh... has a wide range. Um... would you excuse me for a moment? I need to wash my hands." She said clumsily.

"Certainly." He nodded, gesturing to his assistant to help her with her chair. The waiter walked to their table, tray in hand, and started serving the soups.

∞ ∞ ∞

"Oh, God. Oh, God." Harmony rushed into a stall.

"Hello?"

"Joy, you tried to kill me," Harmony yelled, as she flushed to avoid leaving a smell.

"What?"

"I took..." she trailed off. "I ate those death cookies and now...Oh my. My stomach." She clutched it again.

"You ate the cookies?"

"You left them out, you know I love chocolate. Oh... Lord, help me."

"Crazy, those were for Miles. He's constipated." Joy bubbled with laughter.

"I snuck in laxatives, so he could go." She laughed again. "Harmony, girl, you a mess. Serves you right for eating my stuff."

"If you make me lose out on this job, I'll sue you," Harmony said through her teeth, as her stomach turned again. Joy burst into another fit of laughter.

"Joy, you gotta help me," Harmony said, desperation seeping through her voice. "I'm going back to this meeting, call me so I can say I have a family emergency," she pleaded, clutching her stomach. Beads of sweat started forming on her head.

"No, I'm not lying for you." It took everything Joy had to not burst into another round of laughter.

"Joy... *please*! The Lord *gon'* bless you. I'm your sister, and I'm dying, so it is an emergency."

"All right, all right. I'll call back in five minutes. You better answer," Joy said in between laughter and ended the call.

Harmony fixed her make-up clumsily, straightened her outfit, and returned to the interview, pretend written all over her smile.

"Now, where were we, gentlemen?" she asked, taking a seat.

"Oh, we were..." he gestured for a waiter. "This service is horrible," he complained. Harmony nodded in agreement as she pointed to her phone, to ask for permission to take a call.

"Hello. What, are you serious? Oh, I'll be right there," she said quickly and ended the call.

"Gentleman, there's a situation that I need to address and since you say the service is not up to par... ah... we can reschedule."

"Oh, well...ah... all right. I hope everything is okay," he said. Before he could say anything else, Harmony grabbed her purse and rushed out of the restaurant.

Love, Peace, Joy and... Harmony

∞ ∞ ∞

"Joy…you, you tried to kill me!" she yelled, as she burst in through the doors.

"Ha-ha look who it is. Ms. Bubble Guts." Joy pointed, laughing.

"If I weren't so weak, I'd throw something at you." Harmony yelled.

"Try it."

"Where the kids at?" she asked, removing her shoes.

"Miles is upstairs, and Misa is at work."

"Work? She has a job?" Harmony asked, surprised.

"Yes, unlike you, she works." Joy chuckled.

"Don't get mad because I'm *choosing* to find myself a position I love, versus settling at a company for 20 years and being miserable."

"You need to grow up," Joy said, with an eye roll.

"You need to slim up."

"Keep talking, breakable Barbie,"

"You got the Barbie part right…because I'm cute." Harmony flipped her hair.

"Wait, what time is it? Oh, my goodness. Harmony, you're *bout* to make me miss Dave." Joy face palmed and checked the time.

"Dave? Did you get a new boo?" she asked, wiggling her eyebrows.

"What? No. He's my friend from work. He's coming over to pick up the Crock-Pot. I gotta run to the basement to get it. Look out for him," Joy said and walked out.

"Alright." She plopped her feet on the table and rested her back. About five minutes into her quality rest time, the sound of a loud knock pierced her quiet time.

"Who is it?" she looked through the peephole and was met with a man in disheveled, hippie clothes.

"Just open the door!" the man yelled.

"What? Joy, there's a man at the door."

"Well, who is it?" Joy yelled.

"I don't know, it's a homeless man. He's saying open the door. Ahhh... I don't live here. I'm just visiting. I don't have any money," she yelled.

"Open the door!" The knocks became louder

"Ahhh... Joy!" Joy rushed upstairs and opened the door. Dave was already rolling in laughter.

"Harmony, it's just Dave. Hey, Dave." Dave smiled and laughed.

"See Harmony, it's just Dave." Joy chuckled.

"She said she didn't live here." Dave bent down, laughing. "Oh, I ain't had a good laugh in months."

"Oh, ahh… Hi." She extended her hand.

"Here's the Crock-Pot. Tell the fam I said hello."

"Will do," he said and continued laughing as he walked out.

"I'm glad you're amused. First, you try to poison me. Then, you turn me into a potential murder victim. You are trying to kill me, aren't you?" Harmony yelled, as soon as Joy closed the door.

"What?" She laughed. "I told you Dave was coming over."

"I didn't think he was going to look like that."

"Like what?"

"You said he was from work; you work in an office. Why is he dressed like he from the '70s? He got a long beard, stringy hair. I'm thinking he's asking for spare change, he's screaming open the door. Who comes to somebody's house and says that?"

"He thought you were me." Joy laughed again, as Harmony pouted.

"Whatever, I'm going home."

"Harmony."

"Don't Harmony me. You and your crazy friend both need Jesus."

Chapter 8: Stay Woke

This L, talk." L paused his video game, and picked his phone up.

"Hey, L, how you been?" the caller giggled, making Love frown a bit.

"I'm good, who is this?" He took a sip of his Red Bull and rested into the chair.

"Baby, it's me," she whined.

"Look, I gotta get to practice. Who is this?"

"It's Hennessey."

"Who?" He ran a hand into his hair. He searched his memory quickly for a Hennessy, but got nothing. He took another sip of his Red Bull.

"You know…" she trailed off, hoping he'd remember. "The girl from Ken's," she finally added.

"Right…" He remembered. Short, petite, nice behind, cute face, his brain recalled.

"Oh hey, what's up?" he said, with a smile.

"Well, we need to talk," she said calmly.

"We do?"

"Yes, well …I'm, I'm pregnant," Hennessy blurted.

"What?" he said, unsure of how to react to news he was sure wasn't any of his business. "Congrats, I guess," he finally said.

"Congrats? What do you mean, congrats? We're having a baby," she yelled at him.

"We who?" L laughed, choking on his Red Bull a bit. "Who is this?"

"It's Hennessy Sherill Brown. Your future child's mother," she yelled again.

"Yo, stop playing. You must have the wrong guy. We never smashed."

"Yes, we did."

"Lady, you tripping. I never had sex with you," he yelled back. "We never even kissed."

"Yes, WE did. Then you fell asleep. You don't remember? We were over at Ken's. We got tipsy, and you fell asleep," Hennessy explained.

"What? Now I know you crazy, I don't even drink. You got the wrong dude."

"You calling me a hoe?"

"I'm not calling you nothing. You called me, acting crazy— I never slept with you."

"Well, we will see what the court says."

"Bye Felisha or Hennessy or whatever your name is. Stay off my phone, psycho," he spat and turned the phone off.

"Stupid," he muttered, as he left for practice.

∞ ∞ ∞

"Joy, which sauce did you want me to get again?" Harmony put the phone on speaker and placed it on the cart as she pushed it through aisle.

"Peace got the sauce; I need you to get dressing."

"Which sauce? I'm mean dressing," she corrected herself and re-focused her attention on Joy, from an older man, staring at her.

"Get all of them. French, Ranch, Honey, Blue Cheese, everything."

"All of them? I hope you're paying me when I get there." Harmony mocked. She was still concerned about the older men. Especially the one eyeing her.

"I'm cooking, stop being cheap. Lord gon' bless you," she said, laughing.

"Yeah… mmm. Harmony takes the phone off speaker and places it to her ear. That's weird, this old guy kept staring at me like he knew me or something. Guess I have that effect on people. They are mesmerized by my beauty. Somebody needs to tell him I don't like nothing old but money." Harmony laughed, as she grabbed the dressing.

"Just hurry up and get here, and don't forget the dressing."

"Bye." She powered off the phone and continued to shop.

∞ ∞ ∞

"I got everything, you owe me 6 billion, and I don't want no check," she said, as she dumped the plastic bag on the kitchen table.

"Please, put it on my tab." Joy laughed, as she grabbed the bag.

"Tell them, L." Peace motioned to L. He was pacing back and forth scratching his head.

"This crazy girl called, claiming she's pregnant," L blurted. He focused his gaze on Joy, since she was the eldest.

"By who?"

"By me," he muttered, still focused on Joy.

"Ew," Harmony squeezed her nose, "you don't do the grown folks. I don't want to think about my little brother engaging in grown folks' activity."

"L, what does she mean, she's pregnant? Did you sleep with her?" Joy dropped what she was doing and moved closer to him.

"No." He bit his bottom lip. "I don't... no."

"Why is she saying she is pregnant, then?"

"I don't know." He shrugged. "I went on a double date with Ken."

"Ken that ..." Joy trailed off and went back to her salad.

"That is not your friend. He is jealous of you, L," Harmony said.

"You just don't want me to have friends. Not everyone wants to be lonely like you." He stepped backward. He knew that Harmony would attack him.

"Okay, y'all stop." Peace stepped in between Harmony and L.

"Peace, if he wants to be slow and hang with a loser that's on him." Harmony shrugged and joined Joy in the salad.

"Man, you better get her."

"Y'all two chill. Lord knows I don't like drama." Peace sighed—and went back to her seat—picking her phone up.

"I'm up." L shrugged.

"Wait," Joy paused, "did you have sex with the girl, L?"

"No, I don't think I did. That day, I was exhausted. I went to Ken's. His girl Lupe and her friend Hennessey came over. I didn't even want to see her—I was just trying to relax. She got there, and I knew she wasn't for me. She was too hood. She pulled liquor out her purse and swore every other word. I was being polite. They started drinking, and I went to Ken's bedroom. I fell asleep. At least, that's what I thought I did," he explained. He tried to keep a cool and calm demeanor. Joy would roast him, if she noticed any abnormalities.

"So, she's lying," Harmony said, sounding relieved, as she sliced into a cucumber.

"Well, we should meet her, Harmony."

"For what?" Harmony gave Joy a hell-nah look and continued slicing. "See, I'm not meeting no future Maury guest."

"Harm, stop." Peace burst into laughter.

"Listen, I'm tired of paying for kids I didn't help create."

"Harmony," Peace warned.

"Said the woman who won't keep a job."

"Hey, that's my unemployment from when I work." She laughed before saying, "No, I'm joking, I love the children."

"So, I should meet her?" L sighed and pushed his hands deep into his pockets.

"Yes, set it up. We'll be there with you," Joy said, with a warm smile.

"Okay," he said, as he grabbed his cellphone.

Chapter 9: With A Friend Like You...

*J*ust think, we're both getting married this year." Joy beamed, her eyes glistening.

"I know, too bad Harmony doesn't have anyone."

"Peace, Harmony don't want a man. They ain't built the perfect man for her highness."

"Well," Peace laughed, "I remember her thinking Boris Kodjoe was cute," she said softly, as she checked a strapless dress out, making Joy frown.

"Well, Nicole thinks so too, and she ain't going nowhere." Joy burst into laughter.

"What y'all cackling about?" Harmony raised a brow as she entered the bridal boutique.

"Nothing, you finally made it," Peace said, without looking away from the wedding dresses.

"Ooh, this is perfect, Ronnie will love this." Joy removed a pearl necklace from the mannequin—her full lips smiling widely, like their expansion had no limit.

"So will his P.O. officer," Harmony said flatly.

"Why you got to start?" Joy said, without letting her smile falter. "You're just mad you ain't got a man."

"Yes, Joy, I'm mad I won't be on an episode of Love After Lockup." She laughed, as she pulled a dress out of the rack and showed it to Peace. Peace shook her head. She put it back and continued browsing.

"In all seriousness, has anyone talked to L?"

"I did. He is going through a lot of emotions, but he said he's going to step up if it's his."

A young woman with a pixie haircut approached them, her black skin standing out of her sleeveless red dress.

"Are you finding everything alright?" she asked with a smile that looked too fake.

"Yes, we're finding everything okay," Harmony replied.

"Her name is really Hennessy? Can't believe she trapped our brother."

The sales representative dropped her clipboard on a nearby table—her hands balled into fists—and her eyes thinned.

"You Okay?" Peace asked, placing a hand on her shoulder.

"Yes, I'm fine. If you don't mind me asking…who's your brother?"

"Love, but we call him L," Harmony replied, as the sisters dropped everything and focused on her.

"L. L is your brother?"

"Yes," Harmony nodded, "you know him?"

"Oh, my goodness." She gasped, her fists growing tighter. "I can't believe she's actually going through with it."

"What?" Joy asked, already getting impatient.

"Don't say nothing," she placed her index finger on her lips, "but I know Hennessy. Promise me you won't tell."

"We promise." Peace smiled sweetly.

"Talk," Harmony said. She was getting a little angry at her dramatic reaction.

"Well, L's not the father. I'm cool with her sister, Alize, and I overheard them talking about it. They were laughing about how they would trick L. See, Hennessey and her best friend, Lupe, went on a double date," she explained. She paused for a bit to check if her boss was close.

"Lupe got drunk and passed out. L fell asleep, but Ken and Hennessy slept together."

"What the huh?"

"OMG," Peace said, unsure of how to react.

"That's just nasty." Joy made the sign of a cross and kissed her fingers.

"Does Ken know?" That was what Harmony was really interested in. She was set on proving that Ken is scum.

"Yes, he told Hennessey that she had to figure something out. She told him first. That's when he was like, L was there. She said she didn't sleep with L, but Ken was like, he doesn't know that."

"That no-good loser." Harmony gritted her teeth. "Trying to frame my baby brother."

"Don't say I said nothing, okay?" She clutched her clipboard, looked left and right, then smiled.

"You have our word. We won't say who told us. Thank you," Joy assured her.

"Thanks." She placed her board under her arm and walked away.

"We gotta let L know what's going on," Peace said, as she returned the dresses she removed from the rack.

Joy whipped her phone out and texted.

L: *Family meeting at my house. It's important!*

"We'll take all of this." Peace placed the items on the counter and faced Joy. "We got to go save our brother."

"Great!" the representative said with a smile.

∞ ∞ ∞

"Love, we have something to tell you." Joy motioned for L and sipped her Coke.

"What's good?" he greeted, taking a seat.

"She's isn't having your baby," Joy started. "She is setting you up."

"That's right." Harmony couldn't wait to enter the conversation. "Your no-good friend Ken, and Hennessy are trying to play you," she said, with a smug smile.

"Turns out you were right. The night at Ken's house, you fell asleep, and so did Lupe. Then Ken and Hennessy slept together. She told Ken she was pregnant, and he told her to say you got her pregnant," Peace explained the whole situation.

"What?" L yelled, sitting up from his formerly slouched position.

"It's true." Harmony tried to keep herself from smiling. She loved L, but that no good Ken had to go.

"Who told you that?" He stood up, facing Harmony.

"We can't tell you where we got the info, we're sworn to secrecy." Peace raised a brow at him; she wasn't ready for another Harmony-L drama.

"You're accusing my best friend from kindergarten of setting me up, and you can't tell me who said it?" He laughed.

"L, it's true," Joy said softly.

"I want to know who said it. Give me a name." He faced Harmony squarely again.

"We can't." Peace knew he had Harmony in mind. She had to kill that doubt, without giving the sweet sales representative away.

"Then I can't believe it. It's a lie." He moved closer to Harmony. "You probably made it up; you never liked Ken."

Harmony's face fell, a look of hurt replacing her previously triumphant one.

"You think I would do something like this to hurt you?" she whispered; her voice almost not audible.

"You're my brother, I love you. I would never purposely hurt you. We ALL we got! L, we're not lying." She looked at Peace and Joy to back her up.

"Whatever," he vented as he got up. Harmony watched him, a tear streaming down her face as he slammed the door.

He walked to his car, his head down, as he muttered silent cusses under his breath. He snatched the door open and sat in the car.

"Lord, help me," he cried out, gripping the steering wheel.

"God, ahh, that's my friend. God why would he…nah. God reveal to me the truth." He looked up; an angry tear dropped from his eye.

"What?" he muttered under his breath. The only reason he answered Ken's call was to get the truth.

"What? What's up with you."

"Nothing, just trying to sort through something." His palms balled into fists—his teeth grinding.

"I heard that. Hey, listen L, let me borrow $200. I gotta get my car fixed."

"What's wrong with your car?" He tried to sound normal.

"Huh? Oh, I think it's the radiator, or carburetor, or engine,"

"For $200? Who's fixing it?"

"Huh? Ah, this guy I know." He paused. "Man, why are you asking me so many questions? You gon give it to me or nah?"

"I'll bring it now." L turned the ignition. "Where you at?"

"At the Outlet Mall."

"At the Outlet Mall?" he asked, frustrated, as he took a sharp turn. "You know what, I'm on my way." He ended the call and headed for the mall.

∞ ∞ ∞

"You got that?" he asked, looking at his hands.

"Yeah, I got it, but I need to talk to you about something." L couldn't wait any longer; he needed the truth. "Word on the street is you Hennessy's baby daddy?" he asked, his hands balling into fists. He looked at them, angry.

"What?" He was taken aback. "Is she telling people? Man, when I see her, I'm gon…"

"Wait," he interrupted, "you knew she was pregnant by you?"

"Man, listen, L, it's complicated. You know, I'm with her girl—that wouldn't look right."

"You was finna frame me." he pushed Ken's chest. "Have me taking care of a child you knew damn well wasn't mine?"

"It's nothing personal." He shrugged. "You gotta job, and you would be a better father than me."

"My sisters were right. You are a snake," he fumed and started walking away.

"L, where are you going?" he called after him. "So, you gon' let me hold that or what? L. Yo, L we boys."

"I'm not your boy. I'm more of a man than you'll ever be," he spat and disappeared into the crowd.

Chapter 10: Unsolved Mystery

*S*o, Harm, who are you bringing to my wedding?" Peace asked, as soon as she added Joy to the call. "Joy is working on the guest list with me."

"Well, I'm coming with me, myself, and I."

"Her and her multiple personalities are only getting one plate."

"Just remember it's not a buffet, Joy. You have to leave some for the rest of us."

"Not today, y'all." Peace burst into laughter.

"Have y'all talked to L?"

"I did; he found out Ken lied. He is going through, just wanting to be left alone," Peace said.

"Praying for him." Harmony heard Joy making a kiss sound, and she knew she did the cross sign.

"Well, ladies, I'm getting a long-distance call. I'll call you back later," Harmony said.

"Just come to the house, I'm cooking.

"Okay, Joy," she said and clicked over to the next call.

"This is Harmony."

"Oh, Ms. Harmony," Tore said. "Yo, seems you forgot all about me."

"Did I?" Harmony checked her nails.

"Yo, you can't remember the King of NY?" he chirped.

"What can I help you with?" Harmony asked, flatly.

"Wow, so cold. I still want to pay you back."

"You already said 'thank you.'"

"Yo, I'd like to see who I'm talking to. I want to take you to dinner, or something."

"You know what, I have a dinner you can escort me to." A light bulb lit in Harmony's head. She would kill two birds with one stone. Get rid of Tore and shove him in her sisters' faces.

"You do?"

"Yes, my baby sister is getting married, and I'll let you take me."

"Wow," he burst into laughter, "you serious?"

"What, is that too much for you? You catching a flight should be nothing if you're a King, right?"

"Yo, I'd be honored to escort you."

"Great, I'll send you the details right now. Okay, bye." She removed the phone from her ear, but Tore spoke again.

"Wait, are you hanging up? Remember, I called you?" he asked, hoping she'd stay longer.

"Well, I have a prior engagement I must attend. Honestly, I can't sit on the phone and chat."

"Ouch!" His voice went low. "Well, I guess it's goodbye."

"Right," Harmony said and ended the call.

∞∞∞∞

"Guess who has a date for the wedding?" Harmony danced around the table, where Joy and Peace were working on the guest list.

"Who?" Joy asked, as she scribbled away on a paper.

"Yours truly." Harmony did a grand twirl and settled on the couch closest to them. "I'm being escorted by a music executive."

"Harm." Peace clapped her hands together, bouncing up and down in her chair. "That's great! I'll add a guest to the list."

"Wait, what music executive?" Joy looked up from her scribbles. "I hope you are not talking about the one crazy hooked you up with."

"Joy," Harmony put her keys down, "it's not like that. He insisted on thanking me, so, I'm letting him escort me." She shrugged, then removed her cute heels.

"Do you even know this man?" Joy shook her head in mock pity.

"Know?" She paused for a second. "Well, how well do we really know anyone?"

"You have never met him, have you?" Joy gave Peace a knowing look, and she said nothing in return.

"I know you ain't talking. How many internet dates have you been on? You didn't know those sociopaths." She clapped her hands together as she said the last three words.

"You always bring up the past," Joy said, as she returned to her scribbles.

"You're always hating. Don't be mad cause I'm dating a boss and well… you…" Harmony burst into laughter to hurt Joy on purpose.

"You're mad because I'm ENGAGED!" Joy waved her ring finger in Harmony's face.

"You two, please." Peace placed her hands over her ears. Their constant bickering always made her life impossible.

"Anyway, this letter came here today that's kind of weird. I wanted to wait till L got here," Joy said, waving the letter in both women's faces.

"How are my beautiful sisters?" L greeted as he walked in with a smile on his face, which made Harmony happy.

"See, he knows how to treat his sister." Harmony stood up to welcome Love. "Hey, brother." She pulled him into a hug.

"My favorite brother," she mused, messing his hair up.

"He's your only brother." Joy sneered. "Well, y'all Crazy Betsy, sent me a letter. It says that there's a man who claims to be one of y'all father. She said she wants us to call her."

"Why you say one of y'all? What about you?" Harmony pulled away from L.

"Now, everybody knows I look just like my daddy."

"True." Peace nodded in agreement.

"Well, I'm just naturally cute, so I don't know what to tell you." Harmony shrugged.

"Well, it can't be me. I'm my momma's child, and I gotta be Dad's," L added, as he bent to see what Joy was scribbling furiously.

"Hey, I'm Dad's, too. Y'all can be the other guys." Peace turned back to her list.

"Well, we don't want to get daddy in an uproar. We'll just take a DNA test," L suggested.

"How the heck we supposed to get Daddy's DNA?" Peace almost started laughing.

"When Joy goes to visit next week, she can get his DNA when he puts his drink down or when he goes for a nap," Harmony said, without looking up from her nails.

"Who ARE you?" L watched her with horror as he took dramatic steps away from her.

'What?" She looked up. "I watch Law & Order SVU."

Love, Peace, Joy and... Harmony

"I'll do it, but if I get caught…we all go down together."

"Speak for yourself, Joy. Don't get caught," Harmony said in threatening tone, and Joy burst into laughter.

Chapter 11: A Night to Remember

The day of the wedding arrived. Peace was getting ready with Joy at the resort. Harmony picked up Tore from the airport. She hugged him. He kissed her.

"Hello to you too," Harmony muttered, shocked, after Tore placed a feather-light kiss on her cheeks, during their hug.

"Yo, forgive me. You're just so beautiful." He blushed, as she pulled away.

"Thank you. L was supposed to grab you, but he's running around. Long story short, I'll take you to the hotel." Harmony smiled, as he adjusted his luggage.

"No dinner first?" He pulled the luggage and followed Harmony.

"N-E-ways," Harmony said, in between fits of laughter.

∞ ∞ ∞

"This cop is following me," she said to Tore, without taking her eyes off the road. She had noticed earlier as they entered the expressway, but she brushed it off.

Tore looked back, but Harmony stopped him. She kept driving, hoping the cop would go away.

The lights turned on, and Harmony pulled over.

"What did you do?" she muttered under her breath, as she checked to ensure she had her seatbelt on.

"Me, nothing," he said in a small voice. "I just got here, what'd you do?" He raised a brow up.

"Nothing. They must have the wrong person." She aligned the tires and turned the car off.

"License and registration," the officer said, as soon as she rolled the window down.

Harmony reached for her license. "Officer, why did you stop me?"

"I'll ask the questions." Harmony passed her documents to him. He checked it and left.

"You know there's a warrant for your arrest, right?" he said, when he returned.

"Yeah, right." Widened eyes. "For what?"

"Suspended plates, theft. Ma'am, step out of the car, so we can talk."

"Officer," Harmony protested as she walked out. "I didn't do anything; my license can't be suspended. I don't do crimes. Honest, I have never stolen anything in my life. I'm usually the one that gets robbed—this is crazy!" she yelled, as he opened his handcuffs.

"I have a wedding to go to in a few hours," she cried as he cuffed her.

"You can go downtown to explain," he said, as he escorted her to his squad car.

"Downtown, what? I can't do jail, I'm too cute for jail." She kicked, when he pushed her in.

"Officer, is everything alright?" Tore stepped out if the car.

"Your girlfriend's going downtown. You can follow us," he said as he walked back to his car, leaving Tore dumbfounded.

"Officer, can you move your seat up?" She adjusted her legs. "My legs are kind of long."

"Ma'am, it's not meant to be comfortable." He laughed, as he turned the ignition.

∞ ∞ ∞

"Officer, is this Candid Camera?"

"Huh?"

"Am I being Punked? You know…is Ashton going to run out?"

"No, ma'am, you're not being Punked." The other officers burst into laughter.

"I can't believe this is happening," she said softly, sinking into her chair.

"Let's see all the charges. Here, it has suspended plates, toll violations and…"

"What? I've never violated tolls, that's a mistake," she insisted.

"Ma'am, you'll have your day in court to explain. To walk today, it looks like you have a $2,000 bond."

"You want $2,000…Ttt… Today? Is that in Rupees or Pesos?" she asked hopefully.

"Relax." He chuckled—mocking her. "You pay $200, and you can walk."

"Do you take credit cards?" Harmony sighed.

"Yes. Oh, you're using a credit card. That's an additional $20." He smiled sweetly and scribbled something into his notepad.

"What! You know what… I don't care, I'll pay it. Just get me out of here."

The officer smiled and walked to the counter to process it.

"Well, well, well—aren't you the interesting one?" Tore clapped, as Harmony walked out of the station, her hair and makeup messed up.

"This never happened." She shot him a death glare, as she walked to her car. "I don't know what's going on. This is crazy."

"Yo, you a Thug Girl, I'm gon' call you Gangsta Boo."

"And you'll be calling yourself an Uber."

Tore laughed. "I'm just kidding."

"I don't play like that." She sighed, as she unlocked the car.

"My bad, beautiful." He bowed.

"I'll deal with this later; we need to get ready for the wedding. I gotta get there. Peace needs me." She jerked the car to life without regard to her suspended license, motioning to Tore to use his seatbelt.

"And just like that, she's back on hustle mode." He chuckled. "Yo, I'm feelin you."

"Whatever." she sighed.

∞ ∞ ∞

"Joy, where's Harmony? She said she was going to be here," Peace asked Joy—pacing back and forth.

"You know Harmony, she probably got caught in traffic. If she said she's coming, she's coming. You know she wouldn't miss a photo-op–"

"Hello, my beautiful sisters," Harmony interrupted Joy. "You look amazing, Peace," she said, embracing her.

"Harm, where have you been?" Peace asked. She felt her heart slowing to a normal rate—she would've died if Harmony didn't make it.

"Preparing for my… I mean your special day." She chuckled. "Besides, these photographers need me." She did a twirl and laughed.

"I mean, you need me." She laughed again.

"Lord, here she goes. You're not coming to my wedding." Joy shoved Harmony slightly to help Peace fix her hair.

"I'm so nervous," she whispered to Harmony, who gave her an assuring nod, and squeezed her hands.

"Let's pray," Joy said, and they all bowed their heads.

"Father God, we ask for peace today, on Peace's day. Lord, grant our family unity as we join with her new family. Bless her marriage to Alan. Thank you for bringing us together to witness this blissful day. In Jesus' name. Amen."

"Amen," Harmony muttered.

"Amen, thank y'all. I'm ready. I feel better." She took one last look in the mirror and did a twirl for her sisters.

After the wedding, the guests moved to the reception hall. Peace threw the bouquet and it landed in Harmony's hands.

"May I have this dance?" Tore mustered his best gentleman voice, bowed, and asked Harmony to dance.

"Yes, you may," she said with a sweet smile.

As soon as she said yes, he pulled her into his arms, and she fit there perfectly.

They moved left, right, then left again. Harmony felt at peace in Tore's arms as she leaned into his chest, so much that she didn't see XL walk in. Tore moved his hands to her waist, and she allowed him—moving like a graceful firefly.

"May I cut in?" XL said with a smirk, after greeting Peace. He watched for a while, as Tore grabbed Harmony.

"XL?" Harmony gasped. "What are you doing here?"

"You thought I was gon' miss Peace day?"

"I didn't know she invited you." She let go of Tore.

"She didn't, L did."

"Umm-hmm." Tore cleared his throat awkwardly.

"Oh, XL," Harmony remembered her partner. "this is Tore, he is a music executive from NY."

"I'm her date. Yeah, I talked to Platinum. Yo, I tried to get you on Summer Jam, but the promoters changed venues. Yo, I think it was zoning issues." He extended a hand to XL, who just starred at it.

"Music executive? I've been in the game for over twenty years—I don't know you."

"I travel in elite circles."

"I'm a Legend—Living Legend," XL said with a smug smile.

"Mmm... looks like they are about to exit the reception. Let me go see my sister off," she muttered to herself.

"Tore, can you go get my things, please? XL, I'll chat with you later."

"Sure, baby," Tore said.

"Baby?" Harmony and XL said in unison.

"That's what I usually call my girl."

"Ahh... looks like Peace is getting anxious, I better go check on her," Harmony said quickly, leaving the men.

"Your girl? You're not her type." XL chuckled after Harmony left.

"We'll see."

"We will," XL said, his signature smirk plastered on his face.

∞ ∞ ∞

"If you need ANYTHING…" Joy wiped her face.

"If he tries ANYTHING, call me," L said, fighting the tears.

"Right, we on the first flight. Ain't nobody gon hurt my baby sister," Harmony added, pulling her into another hug.

"Y'all, I'm good—God's got me. I love y'all so much." She wiped her face slightly.

"Love you too, sis." L shoved his hands into his pocket.

"Love ya." Harmony pulled her into another hug.

"My baby sis. . ."

"Peace, our chariot awaits," Alan said, with a smile.

$$\infty \ \infty \ \infty$$

"Today has been a long day." Harmony sighed as she eased into the bed.

"You seem tense; you need a massage," Tore said slowly.

"What?"

"Yo, Relax. I'm respecting you, just want to massage your back. These hands are lethal, been known to put people to sleep. Yo, keep your dress on if you don't trust me."

Harmony nodded and got on her back.

"I, Tore Gilliano, want to marry Harmony Wentworth."

"Harmony. Sleep now beauty, we got a lifetime to talk," he said, as she snored away.

$$\infty \ \infty \ \infty$$

"Ahh! What am I doing here? What did you do to me?" Her eyes darted left and right as she checked her body.

"Chill." He chuckled.

"You Mother…" she trailed off, as she checked in between her legs. "Did you?" She swung at him.

"Yo, chill. Relax. I didn't. Yo, you still got cho' clothes on." He pointed at her dress.

"Think about it. If I did something, your clothes would be off. You fell asleep, we talked. Yo, nothing happened," he said, chuckling at Harmony's hard breaths.

"You really are something. It's 3 a.m.. You coming back to bed or what?"

"No, I'm leaving." She arranged her dress.

"Wait, you leavin? Yo shorty, chill." "You tryin to leave me in your city? You buggin."

"Just call an Uber, the airport is not that far. I got to get back home."

"Well, you mind frontin' me. My ATM card won't work here," he said slowly

"What?"

"I tried at the airport, and it wouldn't work. I plan on calling the bank first thing in the morning."

"What the?" She paused. "You know what, here's a twenty. Make it work." She grabbed her purse and headed for the door.

"Yo, call me later to let me know you made it," he called after her, as she walked away.

"Wait on it! She slammed the door shut.

"I can't believe this broke mother. ATM card… people ain't had that since the '80s—lying jerk. Everybody knows that debit card is the term. Probably ain't got a bank account," she mumbled, as she entered the elevator.

Chapter 12: When It All Falls Down

"That no-good mother…ooh. I can't believe Kwame. How did he get my information?" Harmony sighed as they walked out of the courthouse.

"You talk about Ronnie, but Ronnie ain't never had me arrested. Mmh, Lord knows Ronnie changed, and he would never put his wife in that situation," Joy boasted.

"You'll never make it down the aisle because from what I hear, Ronnie on that stuff."

"That's a lie, a lie from the pits of hell—Ronnie ain't never did drugs."

"Oh, he just hangs out with Dope Fiend Shellie for no reason. Maybe he's praying with her at 4 a.m., in the car you got for him, at the meth house."

"Whatever, just be glad I got you an attorney to get you out this mess."

"Ahh… I'm glad it's behind me, but when I see Kwame, I'll be back in lockup—cause I'm gon set it off."

"I'm telling you now…don't call me to get you out," she warned, as Harmony answered the phone.

"Hello?" Harmony's eyes widened, her lips quivering.

"Who is it?" Joy asked, worried.

"My bank trying to verify charges. What the... $5,004.25, $5805.00, $2701.25, $8.93. The only thing I did was the $8.93 this morning for coffee." She pressed one, for the operator.

"This is Amber Wallace #2255, with East National Bank's Fraud Department, this call is being monitored, please verify your password on the account."

"Zero-eight-two-seven."

"Is this Ms. Wentworth?" Harmony put the phone on speaker so Joy could listen.

"This is...I did not authorize those transactions. The only one I made was $8.23."

"I understand your account was flagged, as additional charges were declined. We believe your account has been compromised."

"Wh...How? When?" she stuttered.

"Can you stop in the branch? It appears there was a bogus check deposited into the ATM, with your account number. There were also online charges and looks like numerous transactions in Jamaica."

"Jamaica. What part of Jamaica?"

"Kingston."

"He got me again," Harmony whispered into the air.

"Ms. Wentworth," the representative called.

"I'll be in to change my account," she said slowly and ended the call.

"Harmony, you okay?" Joy placed a hand on her shoulder.

"That no-good, trifling, bastard Kwame did it! This mother, then robbed me and got me arrested," she said, to nobody in particular.

"What? How do you know it's him?"

"Charges were made in Kingston, Jamaica. Kwame stopped by my house and mentioned he was headed to Kingston, Jamaica. He had to take my mail.

Remember, the new checks with the cute logo that I never received…well, now I know why."

"Dang!" Joy muttered, unsure of what to say or how to react.

"What else could go wrong? We gotta get to the bank." Harmony dialed her phone and tried to call Kwame, but his phone was disconnected.

"Funny you mentioned Kingston, Jamaica. Alexandria posted some pic with her and some guy in Kingston, Jamaica recently."

"Let me see your Facebook, you know I deleted my account, since she kept stalking me?"

"See, here." Joy opened the page.

"OMG, Joy, that's him." Harmony gasped.

"That's Kwame?" She cooed. "Girl, he fine."

"You mean to tell me that psycho b…Lord, forgive me, is spending my money with my Ex who just robbed and got me arrested. What kind of…I told you that girl was crazy. She wants to be me So BAD! I didn't even know she knew him!"

"Wow…" Joy said, lost for words.

"If I ever come up missing… check her trunk. Oh, they want to play with Harmony. We gon' play today, they're going to jail, save them pics."

"You can't write this." Joy laughed as she strolled to her car.

"Hello?"

"Hey, Boo, why you sound so sad?"

"XL, they robbed me."

"Who robbed you? You good?

"This dude, name Kwame, and psycho Alexandria down in Kingston, spending money he stole out of my account. He took my checkbook when he came over and made bogus transactions."

"What?"

"Then, he got tickets under my name in a car he registered. They arrested me the day of Peace's wedding. I had just got out when I saw you. So, Joy tells me that Alexandria is down in Kingston, too. She shows me a Facebook pic, and Alexandria is with Kwame."

"You know where they at right now?"

"In Kingston, Jamaica. I told you."

"Do you know where about? Send me the pics."

"I'm not friends with her, Joy is. I don't have Facebook, and Joy's at her house. I'm driving there now."

"I think Alexandria is on my page. Hold on." He paused. "Yeah, I see her. She just posted at the Reggaetón Explosion Concert. I'm going to handle it. You need some money?"

"I'm good, I'm just tired. Been one of those days."

"You good. Hold on…that ain't like my baby. I'll send you something. Yo, you still got the card I gave you?"

"Yeah. Is it still active?"

"It should be. If it ain't, I'll send you some more. You know, I told you whatever you want, I got you," he said sweetly.

"Do you, really?"

"For sure," he said, as Harmony smiled.

"XL, I just pulled up at Joy's. I'll talk to you soon and thank you." She was really grateful for XL; he was like her guardian angel.

"Alright, you be careful out there. I'm gon' take care of this for you."

∞ ∞ ∞

"You good Harm?" Peace asked.

"Best believe, I'm going to be. I'm still shocked," she said, taking a seat.

"That's messed up, Sis. You need me to handle it?"

"Thanks, L. I'm good."

"The Lord will take care of everything; it will all work out," Joy said, as she sliced away.

"You said it," she chirped.

"Oh, speaking of which, I got each of our test results. This will prove Crazy Betsy was just talking. I'll open my results first." She tore the envelope open and dived into the content.

"What's it say?" Peace questioned anxiously.

"Wait, Peace, I'm reading. There, 99.98 %. See, I told you. I knew I was my Daddy's child." Joy burst into laughter. "Who's next?"

"We will go by age. That means you're next Harm."

"Speak for yourself, I still look good." She burst into laughter. "Okay, here are the results."

"What's it say?"

"Dang let me read, Nosey Rosy." Harmony gasped. "It says prob-ab-abil-ity of paternity, 0%. Haaahh... Joy, what does this mean? Is this serious? What the hell are they talking about?" She panicked.

"Let me see." Joy collected it.

"OMG." Peace's mouth hung open.

"Nah, can't be." It was L's turn to gasp.

"She's right, there's no way," she said, passing the letter.

"OMG, I'm the milk man's child, ring twice on Tuesday. This is not my life. What the…I was robbed, set up by my ex who is with my stalker spending my money, and now, I ain't who I am. This is the worst day of my life," she whispered. Her siblings rushed to hug her—tears falling down their cheeks.

"You know what, it's probably wrong. People make mistakes all the time. I'm Harmony, Harmony Wentworth. I'm feeling kind of… of exhausted. I've had a very long day. So, forgive me, I'm going to retire for the evening. Send my love to the kiddies when they get back."

"Harmony, wait.!" L called for her, but she was already on her feet.

"Don't go," Peace whispered.

"Oh my…I can't believe it, I'm so sorry." Joy moved away from them, and broke down in tears.

∞ ∞ ∞

"God, WHY?" Harmony pulled over, as the emotions were overwhelming her.

"Help me, Lord, please," she said in between sobs.

"PLEASE! I just don't …WHY. Lord HELP ME! I can't take anymore. It's not true, it's not true. I just have to go to sleep. When I get up in the morning, this nightmare will be over." She wiped her eyes furiously, and started the car.

Chapter 13: Something's Not Adding Up

*W*ow! So many gifts." Peace clapped her hands together—a big smile on her face. She sat in her room, opening gifts with her mother-in-law, still trying to grasp being a newlywed. Peace thought about Alan's proposal. She could not believe her best friend invited her to his family's costume party, which turned out to be his forced engagement party. She recalled Alan pulling her to the side and explaining he needed her to marry him to stay in the country. Feeling obligated, Peace agreed to help Alan. Considering they never dated, Peace never dreamed she'd marry her nerdy best-friend.

"Yes, weddings are a big deal in my family. You should see the weddings back home. In my country, the ceremony lasts three days." She chuckled as she handed Peace another box.

"Awww! Well, I'm glad we were able to have a wedding, Alan won't be deported now."

"Deported?" She asked, dropping the box she was holding.

"Yeah, you know, I.N.S.?" Peace said, without looking up.

"Why would they deport Alan? He was born at Mercy Center," she asked curiously.

"What? He's American?" Peace gasp, her eyes widen in disbelief.

"Yes," she answered her. The woman was genuinely confused. "How else would he be able to do an Embassy assignment for the United States overseas?" she asked, as Alan walked in; a smile on his face.

"You're AMERICAN?" Peace barked as she stood up to face him squarely.

"What? Who told you that?" Alan asked, feigning confusion.

"Well, are you?" Peace moved closer, ready to swing into action.

"Mom, did you tell her that?" He looked at her and started speaking in Hindi.

"Why would she think you'd be deported? You're second generation." She looked at Alan, then at Peace, and back at Alan. She didn't understand them.

"Peace, I can explain." Alan moved closer and tried to grab her hands.

"You lied to get me to marry you?" she whispered into the air, her lips shaking.

"It isn't like that. I love you," he whispered.

"I can't believe you TRAPPED me into marrying you." She grabbed her cell phone and bolted out of the room.

Chapter 14: Do Not Touch My Anointed

*H*ey, Mon, come dance with me." A rasta girl pulled herself to Kwame.

"Ooh, Come here."

"Come talk wit me here."

As Kwame followed her, he noticed men surrounding him. He sensed they want to rob him. He ran into the street and got hit by a car. He died instantly; Alexandria did not realize Kwame was gone, so she returned to their hotel room.

The next morning, the hotel staff evicted her, and Alexandria went to the beach. She approached a group of elderly men. One gentleman said he was from Florida, and she convinced him to buy her a ticket back to the States.

XL's contacts were at the event, and they told him Kwame is no longer a problem.

∞ ∞ ∞

At Harmony's, she had isolated herself in her bedroom for a week. She did not speak with anyone and refused visitors.

"I just can't believe she won't talk to us. Grief is an intense process. The Kübler-Ross model explains the five stages of grief," Peace said to Joy over the phone.

"You know how she is. I got too much to do at the church to think about your sister."

"Joy, show some compassion; she's going through a lot."

"She's always going through a lot."

"Hello, Peace! How are you lovely?" Harmony called, and Peace added her to their conversation.

"Harm, Hey! How are you?"

"Beautiful, and I feel great also," Harmony chirped.

"Well, well, well so, I guess you're not dead after all."

"Still angry, I see. You're welcome, Joy."

"You're welcome? What? For what?"

"If I didn't live my life, you would have nothing to talk about. Honestly, this must be what it feels like to be famous. I see what Kimie K goes through. It seems I work for the National Suicide Prevention Group. You see...my living saves miserable people's lives. If I didn't live, you'd have nothing to talk about. So...you're welcome, you're welcome, YOU'RE welcome."

"She's back!" Peace laughed.

"You know what, I'm not going to let you ruin my wedding plans with my future *husband!* Me being a Proverbs 31 wife is all I can think about right now. Because I got to get ready for my *husband...* and *our* special day, because being with a Woman of God requires a great man. So, I thank God for my *husband.* "

"Wish you and your *has been,* in-and-out-of-prison, who ain't got-a-pot-to-piss-in, or a window- to-throw-it-out-of the best."

"Whatever!" Joy sassed.

"Oh, you two stop." Peace laughed. "Tell her about the funeral."

"Hmm…well, Crazy Betsy says she needs us to go to a funeral today."

"No, thanks." Harmony said quickly.

"Well… ride with me to a social event. Heard it's going to be single doctors, lawyers, politicians, etc. there. Real money! We'll even pick you up."

"Ok, I'll get dressed," Harmony said and left the phone, excited.

"Joy, why you lie?"

"I didn't lie, all of that is at the funeral."

"She is going to be so mad at you," Peace said, laughing.

"Serves her right."

∞ ∞ ∞

"LET. ME. GO!" Harmony kicked and pouted like a child as Joy pulled her from the car.

"You know we got to show respect."

"Practice what you preach, I'm not getting out."

"You people ought to be ashamed, dragging me down to a death party!"

"It's a celebration of life," Joy insisted.

"Well, why is the guest of honor dead on arrival."

"Look, if you get out, I'll cook dinner for a month," Joy pleaded.

"Thank you, but no. Keep your carbs and cholesterol, Big Girl!"

"That did it, I'm going to slap her straight." Joy launched for Harmony.

"Joy, no. Harm, I have five gift cards from my wedding for your favorite store. I'll give them all to you if you get out."

"Let me see." Harmony crossed her hands on her chest and pouted. Peace handed her the paper.

Love, Peace, Joy and... Harmony

"Well, why didn't you say so? Let me go show my respect. How do I look? You don't have to answer, I know I'm fine." Harmony stepped out of the car. Harmony walked to the front of the funeral, all eyes on her. Guests were shocked she was there. A busy body walked up to her.

"Wow! Harmony…. is that you? Can't believe you here, after what happened at your cousin's," she said, a wicked grin on her face.

"Harm," Peace warned.

"Funny thing, I prefer not to attend funerals. Wouldn't want to mess up my makeup. Looking around this room, I can see this group does not have that issue. This reminds me of a movie I once saw…ah yes, what was it again? That's right, Planet of the Apes."

"Harmony! Let's go." Joy grabbed Harmony.

"What? Did I say something wrong? The Bible tells us not to lie. They *all* look like before pictures."

"Joy, you need to get Crazy Betsy."

"What's she doing now?" Joy sighed.

"She is in a mink coat and a swimsuit; telling everyone she a Queen who can raise the dead," the guest yelled.

"What! Where is she?"

Harmony glanced over and saw Alexandria walking her way. Instantly, she was ready to snap.

"Harm…please, don't let her take you there." Peace grabbed her hand.

"Yeah, Alexandria what's up?" L moved in front of Harmony.

"Hey, L. I wanted to speak to Harmony."

"Now's not a good time."

"Harmony, I just want to apologize. Kwame was cool. I didn't know y'all dated till they did the R.I.P. on Facebook."

"What? R.I.P.?" Harmony gasped.

"Oh, you don't know? He got hit by a car in Jamaica and died. Girl, I had to get a flight from this guy I met. My luggage was left in Jamaica and EVERYTHING. They weren't even trying to pay me back. Girl, it was crazy! I didn't think I would make it back to my kids."

"What the hell are you talking about? You psycho whore! I'm tired of your THOT--"

"Harm! Alexandria take your-dusty-disease invested … you better get away from my sister for it be two funerals up in here," Peace spat.

Joy returned. She saw Harmony, Peace, L, and Alexandria.

"What's going on, L?" Joy inquired.

"Chill y'all." L tried to calm his sisters.

"We family y'all." Alexandria pleaded for acceptance.

"THOT, you ain't no family of ours. You a lying rat, and had I known you weren't REALLY blood, you wouldn't have been around me. Giovanni is my cousin. You targeted me at her funeral when I wasn't in my right mind. That's how you got in. But I'm back now. I'm gon show you better than I can tell you. Let me go, L. She got it comin."

"Let's go. Joy, you grab her, and I got her," L said.

"You two embarrassing yourself. Get it together," Joy snapped, and they walked out.

"I'm tired of that Jezebel trying to come for me."

"Chill Harmony, she ain't worth it. She just wants to be you."

"Lord, Peace, you were supposed to watch her. Not join her."

"Nobody is going to touch my sister. That nasty rat was about to get it."

"Well, Thelma and Louise, calm down. Let's just go back in there and be respectful children of God. For me, please. Between this and Crazy Betsy trying to be a member of the Twerk Team. This is too much," Joy pleaded.

"For you, I will," Harmony muttered.

"I guess we should at least go to the casket to view the body." They walked to the casket.

Harmony viewed the body and gasped. "That's…that's the guy that was in the store. The guy that stared at me." She looked at him and saw their similarities.

"OMG! Harm. This is…" Peace trailed off.

"OMG, y'all favor."

"Ok, well guys, we saw, let's go," she said, then started walking out, leaving the family staring. A flood of emotions overwhelmed Harmony, and she felt like she knew why she was there.

L, Peace, Joy, and Harmony walked to the hallway in silence.

"I just don't understand. This is crazy." She heard someone whispering about their similarities. Harmony was frightened as she walked through the family.

"Can I speak with you for a minute?" A man stopped her. Harmony recognized him; it was the other man from the store. The four of them walked with the man to another room.

"You look just like him," he whispered.

"Look like who?"

"They haven't told you?"

"What are you talking about?"

"My brother, the man we're here for.

"Sir, I don't know *your* brother. I just saw him in the store with you that day, but I don't know him."

"Crazy…I mean, Betsy, invited us to the funeral, but we don't know why." Joy shared.

"I don't want to overwhelm you. Can I have your number to talk to you to explain everything?"

"I can't deal with this right now." Harmony walked out.

"She'll call you. I'll take your number," Joy assured him.

∞ ∞ ∞

"Harm, it's your favorite baby sister."

"Hi, Peace."

"Everybody has been worried sick about you—glad you answered."

"Yeah, I'm just relaxing."

"Let me merge Joy."

"Do you have to?"

"You know she misses you."

"Okay." She waited and allowed Joy to add Peace to the phone call.

"Hello," Joy said softly

"Joy, I have Harmony."

"I can't talk. He's missing."

"Miles?" Harmony gasped.

"Not Miles, my Husband," Joy said, her voice weary.

"Who?" her sisters chorused.

"Ronnie. He's missing; I can't find him anywhere."

"Did you try the Low End?" Harmony said flatly.

"No. Why would he be there?"

"Cause that's where most addicts hang. It's also the day the checks come out."

"You're just jealous! Ronnie doesn't do drugs. I wish people would stop lying."

"Well Joy…" Peace trailed off, everybody keeps saying it. You might want to check it out. I'll ride over there with you, if you're going to check."

"I'll go, too."

"Y'all meet me at my house, so I can prove you wrong. Ronnie is a future Pastor. Sister Retta Prophesied at church, she said I was gon' be a First Lady."

"Bwwwha. Retta crazy, and she prophalied, if she thinks Ronnie is a Pastor of anything."

"Harm," Peace warned.

"Okay, I take that back. I don't know what God has planned for anyone. I'll head to your house right now, be there in a sec," she said and ended the call.

"That girl forever hanging up the phone on people."

"I'm on my way, Joy. Bye."

"Bye."

∞ ∞ ∞

"Ronnie?" Joy gestured for the car to be stopped as she spotted Ronnie at a corner, entangled into the arms of a redhead.

Frantic, Joy jumped out of the car and launched straight at Ronnie.

"What cho' doing here?" he chastised.

"No, the better question is, what are you doing here? I have been looking all over town for you. I'm trying to get everything together for our wedding. They still need your measurements for the tux." She fumed.

"Wedding? What Wedding?"

"What's she talking about Ronnie, you marrying her?" the redhead asked.

"Nah." Ronnie chuckled.

"What you mean, nah?" Joy moved closer and hit his chest. "You're the one who proposed to me."

"I thought she was just your money, Ronnie?" the girl whined. Joy had to use everything she had to keep herself from launching at her as she twirled her red hair in her hand.

"Hush! Go over there and let me talk."

"Who you telling hush too? You don't hush me."

"You know what I mean. Joy gon' go back to the house, I'll be there later." He tapped her behind slightly, and she moved to the side.

"No! I'm not going nowhere without my HUSBAND!"

"Well, when you find him, he can leave, too." Ronnie chuckled.

"You bum." Harmony stepped in. "I know you ain't trying to play my sister for Shellie?"

"Harmony! Go back to the car," Joy yelled, without taking her eyes off Ronnie.

"Uh-Uh, you ain't finna talk to me like that." Shellie rolled her eyes, still twirling her hair.

"Nah, Joy, they not coming for you." Harmony moved closer.

"You alright?" Harmony heard the familiar voice and turned around.

"Huh? I'm good?"

"This mine right here," the man said, facing Ronnie. "Is it a problem?"

"Nah, no problem, we--we out," he said with an evil grin as he took giant steps to the car Joy brought.

"You're not going nowhere in my car. I brought this car." She hurled at him.

"Chill, Joy. Get off me." He shoved her and turned the ignition. Joy, without thinking twice, pushed herself into the car attempting to stop Ronnie.

"Joy." Peace gasped at the sight of Joy's lifeless body on the ground.

"Oh, my," Harmony whispered, tears falling down her eyes."

"I didn't know she was in the door," Ronnie whispered in shock, as he stepped out of the car.

The women hovered over her immediately, trying to shake her to life.

The man grabbed Ronnie by the hand, but he broke loose and ran for his life.

"We need to get her to the hospital," he said as he ran back to the women—panting.

"Call the ambulance, please help!" Peace urged him, as the tears flowed to her pink shirt.

"Joy!" Harmony tried to shake her to life again.

"They'll take too long to get here. Let's get her in the truck," he said quickly and started lifting her body.

∞ ∞ ∞

"We gotta call L." Peace removed her phone from her bag and dialed his number.

"Lord forgive me," Harmony cried out. "Lord, don't let nothing happen to Joy. We can't lose her. Please, Lord! We all we got."

"L, I need you to get to Mercy Center," Peace said quickly. She struggled to keep her voice steady, so as not to get L worried.

"What happened?"

"Just meet us at Mercy Center. I need you to be calm and just drive. We'll explain when you get here. Love you."

"Love you too, on my way," he said and ended the call.

∞ ∞ ∞

"What's going on? Tell me what's going on," L yelled as he ran into the hospital's reception. The nurse at the desk shot him a warning look, and he regained his composure.

"It's Joy," Peace said, without looking up. "Harm, you tell him." She moved aside and allowed Harmony to get closer to L.

"L," she wrapped her hands around him, "she's hurt. Ronnie. The car. He drug her," she said, still in his arms, tears streaming down her face.

"I'll kill him," L said through his teeth as he let go of Harmony.

"He ain't worth it, just stay with us. We need you—we gotta pray." Harmony lifted her hands—tears pouring down her face.

"Hey? Are you alright?" A doctor moved closer to L.

"My sister."

"Come sit over here." She tapped one of the chairs in the reception area, and L joined her.

"I can't lose Joy."

∞ ∞ ∞

"Lord, I can't lose my sister," Harmony whispered as she went down on her knees. "God, please heal her. I plead the blood of Jesus over Joy. Father, you said by your stripes, we're healed. I bind anything coming against your servant. In the name of Jesus, I decree Joy will be healed. Thank you, Father. Your will be done. Lord, that Joy may testify of your goodness and mercy. Lord, loose your angels to go forth unhindered by any outside force. In the name of Jesus. I ask and pray. Amen."

"How you doing, baby girl?

"I know she'll be alright; God is able." She wiped her face as the tears poured down.

"I'm here for you. I'm your family. I'm not leaving you.

"Huh? What? I don't."

"Your father was my brother. Call me Unc. I don't mean to talk about this now, but I need you to know your birthright. You are loved, you're a Gilliano."

"A who? What was the name again?"

"Gilliano," her uncle whispered.

"Lord, give me strength," Harmony whispered, as she remembered that was also Tore's last name

"Your father left you the entire North Side."

"What are you talking about? Left me the North Side…"

"Your father was known; he owned a great deal. He ran the entire North Side. He was away for a while. While he was away, I took care of everything. When he came home, he was different. All he talked about was seeing you. That day in the store, he wanted to speak to you. He was afraid he'd scare you. After that day, all he did was talk about was seeing you again."

"He did?"

"He loved you. He tried to see you years ago."

"Wait. I remember when I was about five or six, something weird happened. My mother told me to go outside with her. The other children couldn't go. I remember being in a parking lot. A group of people were conversing. A slender man with an afro approached us. He had on a white shirt and blue jeans. I remember my mother pushing me forward, like she was showing me to him."

"I was there that day. Wow! You remember that? You have a good memory."

"So, I've been told. What I don't understand is why no one ever told me.

"You know your mother."

"Apparently, I don't."

"She had an image. Our family is not the best. We live *that* life…so to speak. Unlike them bougie Wentworths, she wanted you to have a better life."

"Right now, I don't know how to feel. It hurts, with so much that's been going on lately. I won't say that I had a lousy childhood. It had its ups and downs, but more ups than downs."

One of the uncle's workers and a frantic woman entered the room.

"Unc. I heard it was an issue. They said you went to the hospital. What is *she* doing here?"

"I was just talking to your sister, Kari."

"Sister? My sister is on the operating table. The other is in the waiting room," Harmony said.

"Feeling's mutual. My daddy only had one daughter, anyway."

"Not sure who your daddy is, but you must look like your momma." Harmony shot.

"Alright now, stop acting Kari."

"Nah, this B come along, trying to take what's mine. She better find another source."

"You ugly gremlin! I'll smack fire from ya." Harmony pointed at Kari.

"Alright, y'all. We fam nah." Uncle tried to separate the duo.

"That troll ain't kin to me." Harmony raised her hands up and moved back.

"THOT! I'm Team Pretty." Kari swung her Brazilian lace front.

"More like Team Peta, ugly as you are," Harmony taunted.

"Kari," Unc warned. "Red, get Kari."

"She better sign them papers. Stay out of our lives, we don't want you!"

"The zoo called; they WANT YOU BACK!" Harmony stuck her tongue out like a child.

Kari kicked and shoved Red as he grabbed her.

"What's she talking about? Papers? What papers?

"Your daddy left you everything," Unc said with a smile.

"What?"

"All his businesses. Money, property, territories, workers—everything."

"Huh? Money, workers? Workers of what?" she asked, facing Unc.

"Your dad…was known. You've never heard of CG? Carleon Gilliano?"

"That's my daddy?" Her eyes widened. "The infamous guy from back in the day, the one who would kill on sight—the Kingpin—that's my daddy?" she asked, shocked.

"Your daddy, and my brother."

"I can't," she muttered, stepping backward. "I can't. This is too much."

"You don't have to decide today, but…your decision will affect a lot of people."

"What do you mean? Why would I decide?" She couldn't look at her uncle. Her face showed concern, and her lips shook slightly.

"He picked you. You're his daughter, his birthright—heir to the throne."

"Why he didn't pick Gorilla Girl?"

"She's not his daughter. He was with her mother for years, he raised her as his. Guess when he could not be there for you, he took her in. She wasn't left with anything other than the stacks in the safe at her house. Your father was…let's just say, comfortable. He made me promise I'd reach out to you. It's your birthright," he said, smiling.

"What you're asking me to do contradicts my beliefs. I'm not in that life."

"I get it. It's not for everybody, but it's yours."

"If I don't decide, what happens?"

"If you wait too long, war will break out. Everybody's in panic mode since your father passed. Everyone wants his spot. If you give the order, they follow it."

"I can't do that. Can you just have it?"

"You're giving me everything?" he asked, shocked.

"You know more about it than I do."

"I don't think you understand what you're giving away."

"I have to be able to sleep at night. I can't know that what I'm doing is killing somebody. I can't do it. My faith won't allow it. I know I'm not perfect, but I am saved. I know I get angry—trust I'm praying God delivers me from it, but that there, I know is wrong."

"I understand. Are you sure?"

"Yes."

"It's shocking, considering I've heard you like the finer things in life— this is not a little money we're talking about."

"Honestly, people don't realize that money is not my God; God supplies my need."

∞ ∞ ∞

"Harmony, L, Peace. She woke up! She woke up!" The pastor danced, as he half-ran into the waiting room.

"Pastor, I didn't know you were here," Harmony said as she picked her purse up.

"Come on, she woke up." He beamed as they walked into the hospital room.

The family rushed into the room where Joy laid. Just like everything that had been going on, it was devoid of beauty.

Harmony squeezed her nose when she caught the undertone smell of bleach on the lifeless grey floor. They gathered around Joy's bed.

"Were right here, Sister Joy," The pastor said, holding her hand.

"Joy," Peace whispered as she sat beside her.

"Praise God!" Harmony cried.

"Sis." L didn't move close. He dug his balled fists into his pockets—his eyes tiny, almost nonexistent. He hated Ronnie.

"Yes. I'm... ah...up. Where's Misa and Miles?" she said softly.

"They're with Mother Rupert," Her pastor quickly answered. "They finished the youth program; we didn't want to upset them. They are with Mother Rupert and her grandchildren."

"Where's Ronnie?"

"Don't even mention his name," Peace spat and pulled a brush out of her bag.

"No, where's my husband?" She tried to get up, but the pastor restrained her.

"Joy, that man just tried to kill you. He is not your husband," Harmony vented.

"No...prophecy was I was gon' be a First Lady, so I know he gon be a Pastor, and we're going to have a family and serve. You just don't want me to be happy. I'm tired of taking care of everybody else. What about ME? I want to be loved too." She cried, sinking into the bed.

"Y'all mind stepping out so I can't talk to Sister Joy?" the Pastor asked her siblings.

"No, Pastor." Joy placed her hands on her face to shield the tears. "Nobody cares about me; they just use me. I'm tired of people hurting me. I deserved to be loved too."

"Sis, we'll be outside." L squeezed her hand and exited the room.

"Mm-hmm."

"Yeah, Joy." Peace smiled and walked out.

"It's okay, Sister Joy. You're not alone. God hears you. You're a good woman of God." He took a seat beside her.

"Then why doesn't anyone want me? I have tried to get married FOREVER! I have had men steal from me, call me every name in the book, sleep with my friends, and leave me. My own father talks down to me. He treats me terrible, and I love him so much. When he talks to me, he does the same thing everyone else does. They ask me about Harmony! Harmony doesn't even like people. They will be right in my face and ask me, "How's your sister doing?" If she wanted to talk to them, they would know. I'm tired of raising other people's kids. I deserve my own. Why don't I have my own family? Why hasn't God blessed me with a husband?" She cried, the tears pouring faster.

"God does things in his own timing. Joy, you're a good person."

"Oh, so now you think I'm ugly?" She pouted.

"No, who said that?" the pastor blushed.

"You said I'm a good person. That's what men tell ugly girls or fat chicks they don't want to date."

"What, Joy, no." He chuckled. " Far from it. I think you're beautiful, I always have. I love your size. I mean. Ah… I mean." He blushed.

"You do?"

"I mean, I didn't. Well…ah… are you feeling okay?"

"Back it up." Joy sat up. "So, you like me?"

"Joy, I'm your Pastor."

"Answer my question." She raised a brow.

"Joy, I'm the Pastor. I don't want to offend you or give you the wrong idea."

"Well, do you, or don't you? I need to know."

"Yes." He smiled sheepishly.

"Yes, what?"

"Yes, I like you."

"Like me, how? Like you like tacos, like you like nachos? Can you tell I'm hungry?" The Pastor burst into laughter and Joy followed.

"Or the infamous "friend"?"

"I consider you a friend."

"Oh, so that's it. I'm the token "friend"?"

"No. I didn't say that."

"What are you saying, Pastor?" Joy asked frustrated.

"It's kind of hard to answer when you keep calling me, Pastor." He burst into laughter.

"Okay, Willard Jackson Stanton III, do you or do you not like me, Joy Wentworth?"

"Yes."

"Tell me, in what capacity?" Joy pried.

"In multiple capacities."

"Just tell me the truth. Please, I need to know."

"Joy Wentworth..." he started, his eyes sparkling. "I see you as my wife, my First Lady, my queen. I see you being the mother of my children, growing old with me. I've wanted you to be with me since the first day I laid eyes on you. You are beautiful to me—inside and out."

Joy stared at the pastor; her mouth opened. She watched him as he said things nobody had ever said to her—at least not honestly.

"I'm sorry, I shouldn't have said that." He sighed. "Forgive me."

"No, it's okay. I'm speechless. I've always liked you; I was just settling for Ronnie because I thought you were out of my league."

"Joy, you're in a league of your own. I know I don't have a ring right now…but, would you do me the honor of being my wife?" He looked away from her.

"Oh my God. Am I dreaming? Praise God! Breathe, Joy. Yes! Ahhh!"

Peace, L, and Harmony rushed in; concern laced on their faces.

"You okay?" L walked briskly to her side, his eyes darting left and right. "Joy?"

"What you do to my sister?" L moved closer to the pastor.

"Praise God! Guys, I'm getting married. He proposed," she yelled, clapping her hands together.

"What?" Harmony asked, shocked.

"I just ask your sister if she would be Joy Stanton. First Lady Stanton," the pastor said, without looking at Harmony.

"Praise God!" Harmony danced.

"Sis, congrats! Whoa." Peace gave Joy a hug. "Great! Now I can help you plan your wedding."

"Thank y'all." Joy smiled. "What the devil meant for evil, God meant for my good." She did the sign of the cross and kissed her fingers.

Chapter 15: Till We Meet Again

*W*ho would have known? All these years Joy has been dying to be married, and she eloped. Who knew the Pastor had it in him?" Harmony said.

"Harm, I'm just glad she found love," Peace said, smiling.

"Thank God, it wasn't Ronnie. I prayed that demon away," Harmony professed.

"You and me both, Sis," Peace said, typing away on her phone.

"I saw he was in jail, again. They about to give him and that girl some real time. You know they robbed that place; he got to get some years."

"I pray he finds God," Peace said, looking up.

"True."

"Oops, looks like Alan is calling." She swiped and answered the call.

"Hey," she muttered.

"Where are you?"

"With Harmony, what's up?"

"Have you told them yet?"

"Not exactly, working on it." She struggled to keep a straight face.

"I don't understand why you won't tell them. I don't get why it matters; I am your husband."

"Here you go." She sighed.

"Peace, I am your husband!"

"You don't think I know that?" I'll talk to you later."

"Tell them."

"Get off my back, I will." she said flatly.

"I mean it, Peace. Tell them today."

"Goodbye," she chastised and ended the call. "Take your time getting married."

"What's that supposed to mean?" Harmony looked up from her phone. "You good?"

"Yeah, I'm fine. It's just a lot going on."

"Like what?"

"Just..." She trailed off. "Oh, Harmony, are those new shoes you're wearing?"

"Typical, Peace avoiding conflict. Mmm . . . interesting it must be juicy." She took a sip out of one of the cups on the table.

Peace forced a laugh, with a small smile. "I love you, Harm."

"Love you too, but you're going to tell me your secret. Hold that thought," she said as she answered her phone.

"Hello?"

"My Essence of Beauty," the caller beamed.

"Hey, XL. How are you?"

"I'm relaxing, performed last night in Cali. I heard about Joy. She good?"

"Yes, she fully recovered. She's good; she got married."

"Word." XL gasped. "To who?"

"The Pastor." Harmony threw her head back, laughing.

XL laughed along. "Well, she does be at the church. He's a good dude, so I'm happy for her."

"I'm happy for her too. She's a new woman. I'm glad her husband found her, and he loves her back. They're cute together."

"So are we," XL cooed.

"Here you go. If we so good together, why you got a stripper popping her booty on your page?"

"Huh?"

"Huh, nothing you can hear," she murmured under her breath.

"That's for the fans." XL coughed.

"Well, tell your fans they need prayer. And tell that stripper, don't nobody want to see her stretch marks. She looks like a Magic City reject—a King of Diamonds want-to-be."

You know, I only want to see your moves." XL laughed. "You still rocking with that goofy from NY?" he muttered.

"Why?"

"You know your boy broke, right?"

"Anywho." She shrugged, like XL could see her.

"His God brother famous, but cha guy broke. He's a conman. He gets women to pay his bills, gives some sob story about an ATM card or credit card or something. Did he try that with you?"

"What? Now you know me better than that?"

"Cause if he did, I'll take care of that for you."

"Like you took care of Kwame, huh?" XL went silent.

"I don't know what you are talking about."

"I bet you don't." Harmony laughed.

"You know, I got to protect what's mine."

"Anyways, what did you want again?"

"Your Uncle reached out to me," XL whispered.

"You know my uncle? How? Since when do you be in the South?"

"Nah, not the Wentworth's, your other Uncle."

"What other uncle?"

"The Gilliano one."

"What?" Harmony gasped. "Where'd you get that from?"

"The streets talk."

"The streets... what? People are talking?"

"Yeah, saying you gotta make some decisions. Northside is waiting for you to decide."

"Decide...I gotta go."

"Harmony," XL called, but it was too late.

"Harm, you ok?" Peace asked.

"We need to go to visit Joy, I need to talk to her," Harmony said, without looking at Peace.

∞ ∞ ∞

"You're so funny." The doctor smiled, punching L's shoulder. Ever since they met, they hung out and talked daily.

"I try to be." He removed his phone from his pocket and swiped it open.

"Checking for your girlfriend?"

"I don't have a girlfriend. I keep telling you that. It's my sister. We're meeting up to talk later."

"So, you're really close to your sisters?" She lifts her coffee to her mouth.

"Yep, we all we got."

Love, Peace, Joy and... Harmony

"Wish my siblings and I were close like that."

"They will really like you."

"Oh, does that mean you want me to meet them?" she asked, her face turning red.

"For sure."

"Is this something you do regularly?

"What?"

"Have your sisters meet the latest girl. To check her out?"

"No, you'll be the first one they meet since I've been grown."

"Really? Aww...so I'm special."

L laughed. "Yeah, so far so good. Definitely a keeper," he whispered into her ear.

∞ ∞ ∞

"Harm, are you getting out?" Peace asked as she pulled up at the store on the way to Joy's house.

"Um, let me make a quick call. I'll wait in the car," she said, dialing Tore's number.

"Hello," he whispered.

"So?"

"Yoooo...hello." He beamed.

"Tore, so, what do you do for a living again?"

"I told you, I'm a music executive."

"Mmm-hmm."

"Why you ask me that?"

"No reason, how have you been?"

"Missing my baby?"

"Did you put out an Amber Alert? I heard they find kids fast these days."

"Yo, you wildlin. You a real comedian."

"I try. Mmh, question...do you know a lot of Gillianos?"

"Ahh, yeah… my family. Why, what's up?"

"You know somebody named Juan Gilliano or Ronnie Gilliano or Carleon Gilliano or Keith Gilliano?"

"I heard of Carleon. The other ones, nah."

"Oh, you related to Carleon?"

"No, I wish. He was a legend; he died not too long ago. Why are you asking about him?"

"No reason. That's what it was. I heard his name and thought of you. I knew the name was familiar. I'm trying to give my condolences if you were related to him."

"Oh, nah. He wasn't ours; we're Dominican and Haitian. Our people stay in the islands, Yonkers and Queens—NY mostly. We got here and never left."

"I see. Well, my sister just got back, got to go."

"Wait, what about us? When are we gon' kick it again?"

"Oh, I got a man now. He crazy too. He just got out. Yep, he not scared to go back either. He's the type the check my phone records. So, if you get a crazy call, just hang up. I don't want him to kick your door in. "

"Yo, girl, you wild. I can't have trouble up here."

"Bye, Felipe, sayonara, Juan." She ended the call, smirked, and blocked him.

"Who was that you were talking too?" Peace placed the plastic bags in the car and got in.

"A nobody I wish I never met. Glad he's gone. Lord forgive me for telling that story, but I never want to see that lying bum again. XL was right about him."

"Harm, why don't you stop running from XL? Y'all make the perfect couple."

"He's in the music business, need I say more?" She rolled her eyes.

"Not all of them are bad. Are you waiting on the Billionaire type?"

"Please, I heard about the one who doesn't give his family money. They had an interview with the grandchild. I believe that all she got was money for a degree. Couldn't be me. I would have told him, "either you gon give me some money, or I'm putting you in a home,"" she sassed, and Peace laughed.

"I wish I would have a billionaire for a grand-daddy, and he tell me I can't have nothing. Talking bout, he finna give some money to charity. Well, I don't know who Charity is, but you better tell the heifer I'm yo grandchild. She ain't getting nothing but a promise. Shoot, since when you know tricks to give more than $500. She betta find a friend, call Tyrone or somebody that give a dang, cause I don't."

"Girl." Peace burst into laughter, as she turned the car on.

"Be like... look here, grandpa, either you gon' give me the money, or I'm gon take it; or hook me up with one of them billionaire friends. Better send me off to the Sultan or the rich dude in Mexico. Think I'm going to be poor and you rich? You living bountifully blessed, and I'm supposed to be an involuntary "minimalist"? I doubt it."

"You Crazy!" she said in between fits of laughter.

"I wish I would sit there, and let him tell me he riding private jets, and expects me to take the bus? He better scoot over. We gon ride together," She burst into laughter, her own antics amused her.

"Nah, I'm Just playing. I get what he is trying to do, but shoot, that's a hard pill to swallow when you got a rich relative." She paused as she remembered her situation.

"You so funny." Peace grinned. "Well, XL is good people."

"The man has been in the game for years, everybody knows him. He is real though, and he got his own money, but nah."

"Just go for it!"

"Wasn't you the same one telling me to wait on marriage earlier?"

"That's different, that's XL. He family." She chuckled.

"We'll see," she said, smiling as she approached Joy's house.

∞ ∞ ∞

"Joy, we're here." Peace placed the groceries on the table.

"That's First Lady Joy," Joy corrected her with a smirk.

"Oh, Lord, here she goes." Harmony sighed, and Peace burst into laughter.

"As a Proverbs 31 Wife, I can offer you the tools you need to find a P 31 husband," she said with a smug smile.

"Tell that to somebody who doesn't know you." Harmony rolled her eyes.

"Ok, you two." Peace laughed. "Where's L?"

"He's in the kitchen. Misa and Miles cleaned before they left. They love spending time with Mrs. Rupert, which is something I need to talk to y'all about."

"Ok, I grabbed my plate, so everybody who has something to share… share."

"Harm, you crazy," Peace said, laughing.

"Well, I met a woman." L averted his eyes from his sisters.

"Really, L? When?"

"At the hospital." He couldn't help the smile forming on his lips.

"Who, the doctor?" Harmony pushed a full spoon into her mouth, eyeing L critically.

"Yeah." He beamed, starry-eyed. "She's perfect, smart, funny. She doesn't have any kids, she's beautiful, and loves God!"

"Praise God, you better keep her." Joy pointed an accusing finger at him.

"What? No conflict? Wow! Joy, you must really be happy." Harmony laughed.

"Right?" Peace joined her.

"I am. Life's too short. Do you, L."

"You have my blessing," Harmony said sweetly.

"Go for it," Peace added.

"Well, I got a situation," Joy said softly. The smile faded, and she became serious.

"Okay." Harmony caught the change in mood.

"Mother Rupert wants Misa and Miles."

"Whoa." Peace dropped the apple she was eating, to the floor.

"Wow, what are you going to do?" L bent down and helped Peace pick the apple up.

"I'm going to…" she trailed off. "Well, you know we want to start our own family, and Mrs. Rupert is lonely, and they can go back to the old school since they hate being away from their friends. Before you say anything, Harmony."

"What? Me? Joy, do you," Harmony said with a smile. "You've raised enough children to last a lifetime. It's time for Joy to spend time with her husband and start her own family."

"Thank you." She wiped her cheeks with her finger softly. "Coming from you that means a lot."

"My turn." Peace sighed. "Well, it's hard for me to say this."

"Just say it, Peace, no judgment," L said, placing a hand on her shoulder.

"Alan wants to move me out of the country." Tears started falling out of her eyes. He wants to practice in India."

"What?" L removed his hand. "Why would he do that?"

"I can't leave y'all." Peace cried harder. "We all we got."

"Peace…though it pains me to say this because I love you so much… He's your husband. We'll be here if you need us. We will hop a flight anytime you need us, but Alan is your husband. You got to get to know him, as husband and wife," Harmony shared.

"True," L muttered.

"But I don't know anyone in INDIA! I don't speak Indian." She dried her eyes slowly, but the tears seemed to be relentless.

"I don't think that's what they call the language." Harmony chuckled.

"You know what I mean. This is serious."

"Peace, you are gorgeous." Harmony took her hands. "People flock to you. You're good with children. I'm sure there's a place where you can assist Alan or help those who work with him. You will not be alone."

"I'm with Harmony," Joy said with a smile.

"Okay, y'all promise y'all not gon to forget about me?" Peace pouted.

"Never. You're our baby sister. We love you." Harmony pulled her into a hug.

"We love you, Sis." L said, joining the hug.

"Okay, it's my turn. Here goes…Nah….I'm good." Harmony chuckled.

"What? Speak now, or forever hold your peace. No pun, Peace." L chuckled.

"None taken, cause I got joy now." Peace threw L a smile, and they both started laughing.

'Well, we all got love," Joy added

"But, y'all would have none of that, if it wasn't for harmony," Harmony said, and the four of them burst into an uncontrollable fit of laughter.

∞ ∞ ∞

"Hello." Alan walked in as L opened the door. "Did you tell them?" he whispered to Peace.

"Yes, babe. They gave their blessing; they are happy for us."

"Really?" he asked, as he embraced her.

"Yeah, Brother-in-Law," Harmony said with a smug smile. "You take care of my baby sister, because I will find you."

"I will." He laughed at Harmony's threat.

"Me too," L chipped in.

"And me and my husband."

"Oh Lord." Harmony face palmed, laughing. "Here she goes."

∞ ∞ ∞

"Hello." Harmony lifted the phone to her ears.

"Hello, I have been calling you for over a month. It's wild out here, did you make your decision?" Her Uncle said.

"I thought I did that day."

"You must be sure."

"I don't want to deal with this." Harmony sighed, frustrated. " I also got a phone call from someone saying that people knew that…who my father was?"

"Kari broke code, I'm sorry. She's still upset."

"Broke code?"

"She knows better than to tell family business," he fumed.

"So, everybody in town will know? Is that what you're telling me?"

"I'm sorry. This wasn't supposed to happen."

"I gotta go," she muttered and ended the call.

Harmony grabbed her keys and headed for the church—tears falling down her face.

∞ ∞ ∞

"God, why?" she cried as she dropped to the alter. "I can't deal with this. Why? It hurts. I don't even know who I am." The crying intensified.

"Harmony? Are you ok?' The pastor placed a hand on her shoulder.

"They know! They want me to decide. What to do with territories, money, and stuff. Why is this happening?

"Harmony, I'm sure whatever it is… God will make a way. He has a plan for you," he said, softly.

"Who told you that?" She got up, facing him. "Has my sister been talking?"

"No, God told me. I knew you were called when we first met; you're running."

"Yeah. He said He chose me. Why me?" she yelled out, as the tears soaked into her blouse. "I'm not the "churchy" type," she added.

"God chooses who He chooses." The pastor shrugged, with a smile.

"Why didn't He choose Joy? She loves the church."

"We each have our own assignment from God. I ran too, I never thought I'd be in Ministry," he said, helping her up.

"Why can't I just be like everybody else?" she whispered into the air.

"Because God made you. He set you apart, and he didn't do it on accident. He meant when He called you."

"You don't understand what it's LIKE!" The tears started again. "You don't know what it's like to be MEEE!"

"Until you married my sister, she HATED me! Nothing I did, just the fact of how our parents treated her. They always asked her about me. They made her HATE me. She treated me like dirt."

"When I lost everything, she tricked me into moving in. I had nowhere to go, so I went. She was PURE EVIL towards me. She forgets it was my money and Misa and Miles that got her the place. It was hell—I slept on her couch. She purposely tried to tarnish my image and humiliate me. Do you know how painful that was? To have a person you trust try to sabotage your success?" she cried out.

"I mean…when Giovanni died, a part of me left. It still hurts. To know that after all these years, they just pretend to care about her, so they can get attention. Even that bogus "event" was canceled… after her own "mother" ran off with the money. They don't care about her, or the daughter she left behind. Her mother abuses the child for sport. This pain…you don't understand." She clutched her chest. It felt like there was a hole in the middle—a gaping, throbbing hole that wouldn't let her breathe properly.

"I tried church before. They either wanted to screw me, or screw me over. It's horrible! I remember driving to church after work one day. I didn't have time to change. It was Jean Day at work. When I got to the church, the speaker…made me stand up during bible study. She said I wasn't saved because I had on a pair of PANTS. After that service… I left the church. For years, I wouldn't deal with it. When Joy threw me out for telling another "Ronnie" she wasn't home, I had nowhere to go. All I could do was pray. God opened a door, and this lady let me move in." She clutched her chest again. The pastor just sat beside her, watching. He knew she had to let everything out before she would be at peace.

"When I left Joy's house," she continued, "I took a pack of noodles and the Gideon's bible. It was the first time in my life, I read the Word for myself. To know I was saved by GRACE, and not by works. To know that God LOVED me! That he loved ME unconditionally. It was like a burden lifted off me. Honestly, I love my sister—I forgave her. I love each of my siblings, none of us are perfect. It's...It's just a lot. I can't even deal with "callings" or "being chosen" right now. Not to mention this OTHER situation I'm dealing with. I cannot engage in that life. I don't want to deal with that world."

"You don't have to." He placed a hand on her shoulder again, to comfort her.

"They keep calling me to decide," she choked out, clutching her chest.

"You don't have to," he repeated, in the same soft tone.

"They say it's my birthright, and I have to do something or it's going to be a war, and I don't want anyone to get hurt."

"It's not your concern. You're a part of God's Kingdom, not the world's."

"Thank you." She sniffled.

"Harmony, it's Joy calling." He prepared to answer the call.

"Oh, that's cool, you're right. I'm about to head out anyway, nice talking to you." She stood up, cleaning her eyes. "Don't say anything, okay?" she warned him as she headed out.

"I won't," he said softly.

"God, I need to get out of here," she said, as she entered her car. "I just want to start over. I'm going to the airport and picking the first flight out. God, I just need to go. Lord, order my steps. I need you." She dug her phone out of her bag and opened her text group with L, Peace, and Joy.

Harmony: *Hey y'all! Good news. I'm going on a six-month Sabbatical. I'm about to take a spiritual journey. Joy, I just left Pastor at the church. I need you to take care of my things. You have my account numbers; you have total access to everything. Peace, I may stop in India to see you over the next few months. L, congrats on meeting your new boo. I love you guys so much! Send my love to Misa and Miles. LPJH 4 Life... We all We got!*

Chapter 16: BENEDICTION

*Y*ou made it! I hope you enjoyed their story. Your support means a lot, as it allows me to bless many organizations that are dear to my heart. Before I go, I do want to share my faith. For those who may be searching or who need to come back home, pray this prayer:

Lord, I admit that I have done wrong things. Thank you that you died to take away all my sins. Please forgive me. I receive your forgiveness now and declare that I want to live for you for the rest of my life. Come and fill my life with your Holy Spirit. I now depend entirely on you. In Jesus' name, Amen.

If you said the prayer, welcome to the family *(or welcome home)*. The past is gone, live your life free. God loves us! Jesus did not come to condemn us; He came to save us.

Also, visit:

www.Airadas.com

to find my social media apps (definition: websites and applications that enable users to create and share content or to participate in social networking). Understand that I am a *private person*, and trust I have times when I choose to spend time alone, but please know it is nothing personal. I do have the ability to discern and love genuine people. In this day and age, authenticity goes a long way.

Lastly, promise me you will live your dreams. You owe it to yourself and society to follow your purpose. Avoid sitting on the sidelines, critiquing others who are living their lives. Trust me, you will waste many years if you focus on others instead of your gifts. You deserve to be happy. Correction, you deserve to have Love, Peace, Joy and…Harmony. :)

-Airadas

ABOUT THE AUTHOR

Airadas Sivad, better known by the mononym Airadas (pronounced: ay-rahr-das(Spanish) or ir-rah-das (English) meaning: To Anger), is a Creole-American authoress. Raised in a multicultural family, Airadas learned from an early age the importance of seeing an individual for who they are versus the shade they are. Her thirst for knowledge led her to pursue higher education, earning her an Associate's in Arts, a Bachelor's in Technical Management and a Master's in Divinity. A woman of faith, Airadas is a proactive Christian, singer, songwriter, and avid traveler. As an ambivert, she is extremely private but loves speaking and sharing her many gifts with the world.

www.ingramcontent.com/pod-product-compliance
Lightning Source LLC
Chambersburg PA
CBHW051955170626
46808CB00007B/2638